SHOOT FOR THE MOON

A SPACE ADVENTURE ANTHOLOGY

KEVIN CATHY · LAWRENCE DAGSTINE

DEBBIE DE LOUISE · STEVE LOIACONI

LISA DIAZ MEYER · JOSH POOLE

WILLIAM JOHN ROSTRON · JAMES RUMPEL

J.R. RUSTRIAN · TRAVIS WELLMAN

DIANA LEE WOODY

Shoot for the Moon—A Space Adventure Anthology

Copyright © 2022 by JK Larkin

All rights reserved

Published by Red Penguin Books

Bellerose Village, New York

Library of Congress Control Number: 2022921970

ISBN

Print 978-1-63777-337-6

Digital 978-1-63777-338-3

CONTENTS

THE LAST HOTEL ON MARS

JOSH POOLE

"Mortal as I am, I know that I am born for a day, but when I follow the serried multitude of the stars in their circular course, my feet no longer touch the earth; I ascend to Zeus himself to feast me on ambrosia, the food of the gods." –Ptolemy

The words were carved into a metallic monolith that stood outside the building itself. Ray Van Cleef walked past the placard carrying a heavy suitcase filled with the few personal belongings that the shuttle passengers were permitted. In spite of Mars having less than half the gravitational pull of Earth, the hotel plot utilized a centralized gravity coil buried several meters under the lifeless red rock, and this caused the luggage to be just as heavy and burdensome as it was when it was loaded into the craft on Earth's surface.

Ray took a deep breath, feeling the manufactured air fill his lungs. He looked over at the greenhouse area, where thousands of plants produced food for the dozens of guests staying at the Hotel Shalbatana. Ray, however, was just a lobby boy lost in his late 20s, selected for the most expensive operation in human history only because one of the chief investors in the project, Florence Roethke, had enjoyed his services while she stayed at a small-town inn named The Corolla House in rural Pennsylvania.

He checked the stubble on his face, wondering if, perhaps, it was time to shave it all off to prevent any accumulation in the small atmosphere. Body-based pollutants built up quickly in the sterile microcosm of the Hotel Shalbatana, with the filtration systems unable to catch the small flakes of shed skin cells or loose strands of hair. There was an employee, Sarah Sarandon, whose entire job was to take care of such things, but with forty-three people between the guests, workers, and flight crew, the task was impossible.

"Is it always like this here?" The mustached Floyd Emerson asked, adjusting the tie on an antiquated suit from the early 20th.

"Yes," Ray replied. "The atmosphere is closely monitored and fluctuates only by three-degree margins as it compensates for the unpredictable weather."

"Remarkable," Floyd said. "Truly remarkable."

Only the outer perimeter of the hotel grounds was covered in the native surface, with the rest characterized by a synthetic carbon substrate that was smooth, indestructible, and arranged in complex mosaic patterns to emulate the outdated Isidore of Seville's *De Natura Rerum*, with the concentric rings lines with lucid calligraphy denoting the old names. Though out of place among the technology, the medieval foundation lay below the gothic architecture of the hotel, complete with spires, numerous arches, and flying buttresses that defied gravity all soaked in a pearl coloration.

"How long have you been here, son?" Floyd asked, adjusting a fedora as the shuttle ceased to make any noise sans some intermittent knocking.

"Since we opened, so, six years."

They made their way across the courtyard, which was barren of any decoration or monuments with the exception of the monolith and a gold-plated sundial that was poised at the far end near the atmospheric barrier.

"So, you've stayed here longer than anyone else?"

"Yes, Mr. Emerson."

"Floyd," the man corrected. "I paid three billion dollars to stay here, and yet, you've been here for six. How'd that happen?"

Ray explained the situation with Florence, at which Floyd simply smiled with his old face and replied, "I suppose the lesson here is to never underestimate the value of a gentleman's conduct."

They walked through the lobby, which featured no doors due to the controlled atmosphere. The pressurized dome was visible only upon approach, and from within its confines was completely indistinguishable from the surrounding Martian atmosphere sans all the warnings. From afar, however, the barrier resembled a glass case, with the fast-moving particles causing small sparks as they careened into wandering bits of dust and larger matter. During the dome's testing on the Earth's surface, the walls were shown to dispel hurricane winds, and in the low-gravity of Mars, the barriers were slightly stronger.

The barrier was generated by a series of energizing stations, a total of sixteen that had been launched from Earth and buried into the regolith by their impacts. Each of these stations produced as much energy as Earth's largest dams, and concentrated it entirely into the barrier using a series of converters. In spite of the technology they operated on, the fail safes were all archaic, designed to withstand the impacts of implantation and last long after the hotel would be decommissioned. Some of the constituent parts of the machines had been designed over a century earlier.

"I'm staying in room 203," Floyd said as they wandered up the bifurcated stairwell that twisted into two helixes which ran up the full four stories.

"Yes sir."

"How's the food here, by the way?"

"It's not bad. We have a good chef and kitchen crew, but it's just a matter of sourcing ingredients," Ray said with a laugh.

"Well, thankfully I didn't come here for the food."

The second floor began with the first spiral of the stairs, much to the relief of Floyd, who was probably as old as some of the analog clockwork in the barrier machines and only half as resilient. Ray led him to his room, opening the door using the biometric hand reader. The room inside was small, but filled with enough articulate décor that the interior looked like it belonged inside a Fabergé egg. The bed was canopied, with white curtains that tumbled down like four distinguished dresses worn by floating matriarchs.

"Not bad, not bad at all," Floyd said with a laugh.

"They spared no expense with the rooms," Ray replied.

"Well, I think I've got it from here, uh, say, when do they serve dinner here?"

"Three o'clock, in two hours, sir."

"Excellent. Do you know what they'll be serving?"

"Mushroom risotto, asparagus from the greenhouse, pineapple with mint and a house cream, finished with a Nebbiolo. Or begun with a Nebbiolo and finished with another Nebbiolo, if you'd like."

Floyd smirked, sitting down on the bed, and working on removing his cryostasis boots like he was removing a walnut shell.

"Let me know if you need anything else, and I hope you enjoy your stay at the Hotel Shalbatana."

Ray disappeared from the room, the door shutting behind him as if it were sucked in by a phantasmic gust. His footsteps rang out like machine gun fire down the staircase and into the tiled floor of the lobby where the echoes reverberated off the narrow columns and large, vacuous recesses that compiled into the cavernous architecture.

Floyd was the last guest on the current schedule for the Hotel Shalbatana, though Ray paid that no mind as he leaned against one of the columns. The columns themselves were constructed out of a carbon nano-tube structure, one that gave them an iridescent finish whose benthic depths rivaled that of space itself. To the left of the column, with a scent that lightly filled the entire lobby, was a lever-press espresso machine made out of brass and copper, with a cherry wood handle that, by then, was more expensive per ounce than gold.

Ray wandered over to the machine, using a wall faucet to fill the vessel, opened the steam valve, turned on the machine, grinded espresso as he waited for the pressure gauge to rise, filled basket with grinds, tamped the grinds, grabbed a heated cup from the storage unit below, raised the lever, and then slowly pressed it down to cause a ribbon of espresso to fall into the cup. The crema formed perfectly at the top, its velvet froth reminding Ray of how much time he'd just wasted. He exhaled, sampling the piping drink, and gazing across the lobby with Ozymandian pride.

One of the most peculiar aspects about the Hotel Shalbatana is the complete, enveloping quiet within its halls. The atmosphere barrier stifles any exterior sound input, while the structure itself was built with tremendously thick, dense walls that suppressed any noise coming from individual rooms. It was thus to be expected that his light sips upon the frothing surface echoed through the hall, bouncing around like crazy thoughts.

"Was that Mr. Emerson?" A woman's voice asked from behind.

"That was Floyd, yes," he replied.

It was Nora, Hotel Shalbatana's head chef, clad in her white chef's coat but missing the accompanying hat.

"How is he?" She asked, maneuvering to use the espresso machine.

"He's fine."

"No, I mean, what's he like?"

"He's nice, I think. He might've even been my favorite if he'd been here longer."

"What's that supposed to mean?"

"Things grow on you."

"Nothing grows on Mars," she said with a smirk. "Except the spindly fingerlings you call potatoes in the greenhouse."

"Didn't you say that produces a more concentrated, robust flavor?"

"Now why would I say a thing like that?" She finished making her espresso. It came out slightly lighter than Ray's.

Ray laughed, doing everything within his power not to spill any of the espresso from his cup.

"Well, I have to start cooking for dinner. If you don't mind, could you set up the dining room?"

Ray nodded, cradling his cup as he scurried across the hall and through an open doorway. Inside, the narrow doorway quickly sprawled into a massive dining area, complete with five tables that could each sit eight people. He added Floyd to the usual number of dining guests, which equaled thirty-three since the likes of Jacob

Traubert and Delilah Bleech always wanted their meals delivered to their rooms. The other eight people in the hotel were all workers who either snacked throughout the cooking process or would snag the leftovers. Ray's duties consisted of placing silverware and plates, which were already cleaned and sitting in neat piles on an auxiliary marble table along the side of the room. With a sigh, he commenced the task.

The plating of each table took between five to six minutes, resulting in a complete ritual taking up roughly half an hour. There was just under an hour left before the guests would begin seating themselves, usually grouping themselves with the same company they'd been sitting with the entirety of their stay. To the surprise of Ray, Floyd arrived a mere fifteen minutes after he finished placing all the formalities and utensils, standing in the doorway that separated the dining room and the main hall.

"Good afternoon, Ray, it's been a long time," Floyd mused.

"Afternoon Floyd. We won't have any food reader for about forty-five minutes or so, but I could get you an espresso?"

"How about we both get one? My treat, seeing as it's all free now." Floyd did a curtsy sweep with his leg and gestured tantalizingly with his arm.

"I just had one, but I don't see the harm in having another."

Ray joined Floyd to wander out into the hall.

"Now, how do I operate this thing?" Floyd asked, gently touching the handle to the machine.

"Watch me make mine and you'll probably be able to do yours without any instruction."

Ray went through the motions, making himself a shot that he poured into a different cup from the one he'd used earlier. Floyd watched intently, as if he were going to be given an examination on the task.

"I think I got it," Floyd said with a tone that betrayed everything but confidence.

He replicated the motions with precision, opting to do the same as Nora did and simply reuse the grounds for an additional pressing. The espresso steamed in his cup; the light froth formed at the surface with an inviting, nutty aroma.

They stood together, staring away from the espresso station towards the open door that led into the dining room.

"Mind going on a walk outside? Back on Earth I would walk four miles every day, always in the evening just before the sun set. Didn't matter how cold, whether it was raining, I always went," Floyd asked.

"Course," Ray replied. "I don't have anything to do for another half hour or so."

The two men wandered out of the hotel and onto the walk outside. The greenhouse stood, poised on its own stonework while, far to the left and wrapped around the side of the hotel itself, there was a small courtyard where a trellis laced with artificial wisteria leapt over a bench. It faced the Iani Chaos, the 200km mesas that rose in the distant horizon like tightly-woven red columns.

"Looks like a good place to sit and talk," Floyd proposed.

"Best at the Hotel Shalbatana."

"Best in the universe."

The bench was small, but adequate for the two men to sit next to one another and still have some space in between to set their drinks without fear of knocking them over.

"So, you ever been married?" Floyd started the conversation.

"No, never married. I had a girlfriend back on Earth, but we separated. Couldn't do long distance I guess," Ray said with a smirk.

"No, I suppose not. Can't blame her for that though. What about the chef? What's her name?"

"Nora," Ray took a sip of his espresso. "I'm not really her type."

"Oh, come now," Floyd said, patting Ray on the shoulder. "You think she's out of your league?"

"Oh, no, no. She doesn't like men," Ray said with a laugh.

Floyd didn't reply, but smiled and gave a brief chuckle.

"So," the old man said after a long pause. "How many of the guests are departing?"

"Twenty-seven, early tomorrow morning. Before the storm hits us."

"So that leaves sixteen here. Do all the workers know they're going to die if they stay here?"

"Yes, they're all departing in the morning. The sixteen that have decided to remain are all guests, with the exception of course being myself."

"You know," Floyd chuckled uneasily. "I can't believe the planet conjured a storm big enough to wipe out this barrier, and in my damn luck I can only get here in time to watch it dissolve into oblivion after only a night's stay."

"Are you afraid of dying, Mr. Emerson?"

"I've been dying for six years, cancer. That's real death, Ray. This, that flash of hot sand and wind, that's something else. That's," Floyd found himself lost for words.

"Divine?"

"Yes, that's exactly what it is. Divine."

"Why are you staying?" Floyd asked, taking a long sip that, at least from Ray's angle, seemed to wipe out the remains of his espresso.

"I don't feel like starting over again," Ray replied.

"You're what, twenty-eight? That's a hell of a lot of life to throw away. Me, I'm surprised I'm losing more than a few months, but you, you're giving up a hundred years or more."

"It's like you said," Ray said as he leaned back into the bench. "Best in the universe."

They shared no more words with one another, opting instead to stare off into the Chaos as the outermost edge of the distant storm began to manifest over the high cliffs.

LOST IN A LOST WORLD
WILLIAM JOHN ROSTRON

It all went so very wrong. The planning for our space voyage was superb...at least that is what *they* told us. Nothing could go wrong...*they* told us that too. However, *they* will never know how screwed up everything became because all lines of communication were destroyed when we crashed on this god-forsaken planet. *They* will never know that their minute calculations had been for naught. *They* will never know that we all died.

It all started so exceptionally well and with such enthusiasm, even though it would take us three years to get to this nearest inhabited planet. There were six of us, interestingly all male. They never explained that, but the rumor was that they feared an onboard romance (like that couldn't happen with men?) or, worse yet, a pregnancy. As I said, *they* never told us.

Perhaps, more interesting was our designations; instead of using our names (which could be quite long in some cases), we had numerical code names to simplify all messages. Indeed, the cardinal numbers were code for ordinal numbers representing importance to the mission. I was insulted. The pilot and co-pilot were "1" and "2." The ship's doctor, who doubled as a psychology expert and morale specialist, was "3." The Biologist/Anthropologist was "4," and the sociologist/cultural expert was "5." I was number "6," the linguist. Okay, I understand the pilot being "1," but without me, what good were all the others?

I had spent over ten years studying the languages that I heard over radio signals sent through space. I had reviewed them diligently to make myself fluent in the most common languages of this alien planet. I should have been called "Number 2." However, in the end, it didn't matter because "1" through "5" are gone, and there is no intelligent life on this hellhole for me to communicate with. Did our scientists miscalculate which planet the messages came from? Or, on the other hand, did the meteor that hit us on approach knock us so far off course that we did not even land on the world that was our destination? I'll never know. Number 1 and Number 2 died instantly on impact. My colleagues Number 3 and Number 5 lingered a bit longer but soon succumbed to fatal injuries. That left Number 4 and me.

I soon realized that, ironically, we two were the best suited to survive this disaster. Number 4 could understand the physical components of this world better than any of us, and I could speak to any beings we came upon. But, of course, that was my ego talking. Where we intended to go, there would have been intelligent life. Where ended up—not so much. We had detected life forms numbering in the millions, maybe in the billions, where we were supposed to go—most of which were housed in carefully constructed buildings. Yet, looking around me now, I see nothing. No words in my language or the language of our destination planet could describe what we viewed before us. How far off course were we? We wracked our brains for clues to our whereabouts. We tried to reconstruct our final moments in space.

"Readying our approach to the final destination," announced the pilot.

"Roger that," answered the co-pilot.

"How long?" I think it was Number 5 who yelled in anticipation.

"Approach could be a day-long affair," answered the co-pilot. "We must search for the large cities we believe are here."

"Not to mention that those signals could have been coming from the adjoining planets in this solar system. So, I think Number 6 better start monitoring the radio to get a more precise landing location."

That order by the pilot is what saved my life. My communication booth was thickly padded with insulation to aid the acoustic properties of my location. No sooner was I settled in my cubicle than Number 4 popped into the seat next to me.

"You have to see what is...." It was the last words spoken before we crashed. The pilot had spotted an object approaching the ship at a rapid rate. He assumed it was a meteor, but I will always wonder if it was a missile sent from below to destroy us. However, the fact that there does not appear to be any intelligent life down here will forever leave my theory unproven.

Now Number 4 and I found ourselves without food, water, or tools. We had escaped the ship with the clothes on our backs. We had pulled Number 3 and Number 5 from the wreckage, but their wounds were catastrophic. Perhaps, if we had been able to hydrate them or mend their injuries, they could have survived. However, we had nothing, and the person who would have known what to do, Number 3, was one of the patients.

We looked everywhere for water but only found unusual formations. Liquid with beautiful blue color surrounded by a reddish hue on the edges seemed to have the composition of water, but when Number 4 bent down to drink from it, he found out the contrary. He did considerable damage to his hand as he cupped it and dipped it into the liquid. Luckily the burning sensation hit him before he could place the liquid in his mouth. However, his scalded hand immediately began to blister, and we had no way to cool it down. His pain grew as we searched endlessly for a water source to both soothe his wound and quench our thirst. Yet I could not help but notice the beauty of this pool of danger.

We trekked on, looking for something to eat or drink. If this proved impossible, we would surely die. We next came upon a fantastic sight. It was a natural formation but still reminded us of an ornately carved staircase. An entire hill seemed to be flowing with a colorful heated mud sliding down its steps. Water, minerals, and limestone were being heated below the ground, boiling over the top of the hill and flowing down its natural rock steps.

Being a scientist, Number 4 guessed that the main components of this beautiful mixture were water and calcium carbonate, a substance we frequently used at home as an antacid. If we could just find a pool separated from the flowing heated main body, it might be cool enough to drink. So we searched the edges of the vast mud waterfall until we found a small pool in the shade. Insane with pain and thirst, Number 4 threw caution to the wind and drank from it. His smile told me it was safe; however, as I lowered my head to drink, he let me know its taste was horrendous.

Our joy was short-lived. Number 4 now removed the cloth with which he had bandaged his hand. The burnt area had become infected, and it seemed as if it had now spread up his arm. I was a linguist and knew nothing about this kind of problem. However, the look on his face told me that he was in trouble. But, perhaps, if we had medicine…

"It's too late," he whispered. "I can feel that it has spread farther than you see."

"Let's keep going. Maybe we'll find somebody…or something."

We didn't. Number 4 died the next day. I was all alone.

Starvation was driving me to madness. Then, too late for Number 4, I found beautiful fresh flowing water streams. I wouldn't die of thirst. I wish I knew how long I could go without food? I roamed a couple more days, becoming increasingly weak. I passed more pools of the colorful hot water, and at times it gushed out of the ground. Finally, I concluded that this entire planet must be a crust of dirt built over a burning cauldron of a hot core. How else could I explain what I was seeing?

Yet, if there were freshwater, logic told me that there must be life forms…and I was proved right. At first, a rumble in the distance drew me in. Over the hill was something, and it had to be good because right now, anything that changed my situation had to be an improvement.

I was almost crawling because I was so weakened by hunger. And then I saw them. Where had they been hiding for the last six days?

How had I not run into one of these creatures before—and now I saw thousands.

At home, anything that walked on four legs could be considered a food source. These creatures had four legs. However, they dwarfed me in size. They appeared to weigh about ten times my weight and were huge and had dangerous horns on what appeared to be their heads. It was suicide to hunt one of these, but it was also suicide not to. As I grew weaker and weaker, I would not even have the option to pursue the herd.

I found a large stick and looked for one of these animals who had strayed from its group. Perhaps they were docile, killing one would not be difficult. Maybe I could make a fire with some primitive form of friction. But unfortunately, I was getting ahead of myself. At that point, I resolved to eat raw meat just to get my strength back. But were these animals even edible meat?

I approached a smallish one that seemed to be set apart from the crowd. By small, the young animal probably only weighed four times my weight. I clubbed it over the head. I drew blood, but he only stared at me in confusion. It was then that not only did he anger, but larger members of the herd also did. I saw the foolishness of my ways and started to run. Now there were no thoughts of food but rather survival. If I could just reach the tree line.

At first, I was far ahead of them, but they rapidly made up the distance once they got going. As the lead animal closed in on me, I made a sharp veer to the right, and he ran right passed me, stumbling a bit as he did. However, before I had time to gloat at my maneuver, the second one was upon me. I could feel my starvation sapping my strength as I attempted the same move on the second beast. Too slow. One of his horns punctured my right side as he lifted me off the ground and hurled me a dozen feet. Satisfied that they had enacted revenge for my brutality toward their youngster, they lost interest and returned to their herd. I should have been happy that they were not carnivores. However, I was bleeding profusely, and my left arm was at a crooked angle. I soon realized that my desperate action in attacking one of the beasts was a fatal mistake. I knew that I did not have long. I struggled to reach the tree line, hoping, at least, to be comfortable in the shade in my final minutes or hours.

I have recorded my saga on the communications equipment provided. But who will ever hear it? Who will ever come to this horrid planet? Why would they?

I know that I do not have long. My senses are failing me. I swear I can hear people speaking. So, I'll use my last bit of energy to crawl a bit further—to a clearing in the woods.

Is that a signpost? I am a linguist. I have learned the languages of the planet that we were supposed to explore. However, there was no way from radio communication to know what their written language would look like. This sign has twenty-three symbols spaced into three unequal groups. Does that mean it is three words? I crawl a few more steps to touch the sign. The letters are indented, perhaps carved into the wood. My fingers follow the form of the first symbol—two straight lines converging at a point and then proceeding downward as one line. What does it mean?

I hear voices...or do I? I am fading fast. My blood loss is robbing me of any rational thought. Am I imagining hearing the voices spoken in one of the languages I studied so hard to learn? I will leave my recording unit on. Maybe I will have the strength to listen to it later if I feel better. Yes, maybe later...maybe...

"Welcome to your tour of Yellowstone National Park. We will be making multiple stops to see the many wonders of nature. 'Old Faithful' and the other geysers are just part of the amazing displays to be viewed. All of Yellowstone lies on an ancient volcano that creates the fumaroles and mud pots, those beautiful but dangerous multicolor hot springs. And that's not to mention the Mammoth Mud Falls made of calcium carbonate.

Finally, we hope to encounter just some of the thousand Bison who roam the park. However, do not get too close—they can attack, and their horns can fatally wound you. Please be extremely careful out there. Remember that Yellowstone is very different most places on Earth. It is almost like being on an alien planet."

CRUELTY

JAMES RUMPEL

I can't make an accurate guess as to how long we were there. The last of us to try to keep track of the days either gave up or died a long time ago. Most of us were in our twenties when we began the mission and based on my memories of the human aging process, I would say we were now in our forties or fifties. However, it was possible that we had aged much quicker than normal because of the hardships we'd endured.

It is impossible to keep track of time by traditional methods. Instead, we count our time by lives lost. We have been here, enslaved and tortured, for two-hundred-thirty-five lives. Sixty of us remain.

We had come to this world on a mission of peace and exploration. Even with our superior technology we were no match for the sheer numbers the inhabitants of this planet threw at us. Our three hundred scientists and explorers were no match for the thousands of creatures that had overrun our ship within minutes of landing. No one could have anticipated the onslaught.

I sighed heavily, more so because of the emotions produced by my memories than physical exhaustion.

"Charles, sit down and rest. You're going to give yourself a heart attack." Naomi always watched out for the rest of us.

"I'm fine," I replied. "If we don't get the carrier loaded, they are going to punish us. The last thing any of us need is to be beaten or have to go without rations."

We worked in a dimly lit mine, nothing more than a cave. The flickering flames of candles provided sparse light and the reassurance that oxygen was still available in the deep interior of the mountain. The walls were made of dark red and brown rocks with veins of olive-green winding through them. To me, they resembled an old tapestry or map hanging on a castle wall.

"It doesn't matter," added Tom, as he emptied his bucket into the large carrier. "They're going to keep pushing us until we've cleaned this entire mountain out."

The material we mined was a soft pliable metal, light-green in color. We called it snot and our captures never bothered to tell us any other name for it. Except for a few rudimentary hand signals or pointing out a new vein to be mined, communications were kept to a minimum. They never spoke.

I used a small hammer to chisel away another section of rock and knelt to pull the snot away from the hard pieces of stone. Extraction of the material required fine motor skills to grasp the snot and a good deal of strength to pull it free from the rock it clung to. My mangled and arthritic fingers managed to scrape the snot off, but the task was much more difficult than it had been when this all began.

"Something is up, though," commented Naomi. "They seem more agitated than normal. They can't expect the few of us who are left to match the amounts we used to gather."

"I wonder if they're smart enough to figure that out," chuckled Tom. "Their only advantages are sheer numbers and a willingness to sacrifice themselves."

I looked over at our guards. About twenty of our captures stood watch over our small work crew. There used to be more but as our numbers dwindled the size of the guard brigades also shrunk, though they still always maintained at least a four to one advantage.

The aliens, though, I suppose, technically we were the aliens, each stood nearly a head taller than me and carried multiple weapons. The firearms that some of them possessed had once been ours, though our captures rarely used them. They preferred to use the large ax-like weapons they always had at ready. They wore thick, heavy atmospheric suits, blacker than nighttime in the furthest recesses of the mine. We had learned through the years that snot was extremely poisonous to them. Even minimal contact with their pale white skin would be fatal. That is why they needed us to do the mining for them and why they always wore the protective garb.

A watcher stood behind the guards on a platform of rock. It was dressed in similar gear as the guards but did not display any type of weaponry. There was always a watcher, never doing anything but observing.

The horn that signified the end of our shift blared in the distance. The five workers in our detail immediately began to set our tools on the ground. The next set of workers would continue what we had started.

The leader of the guards, clearly distinguished by his heavily decorated ax and his immense size, stepped forward and gestured toward the tools. He raised and lowered his weapon repeatedly.

"I think he wants us to keep working," said Naomi.

"What if we refuse?" suggested Tom. "What are they going to do, kill us?" He turned to face the lead guard, his arms across his chest.

The guard signaled for Tom to continue working one more time. Tom just stood there with a huge grin on his face.

"Tom, I think we better do what he wants," I said.

"He's not going to," whispered Naomi. "He's had enough; he's finished."

If I wasn't such a coward, I would have joined him.

The blow was quick and deadly. The leader again signaled for us to return to work.

We did as we were directed, as we have done for two-hundred-thirty-six lives.

Eventually, we filled the carrier and rolled it to the dumping point. There was no telling how many tons of snot we had collected during our time on this planet. In all these years, we had never been told or figured out what the aliens used snot for. We only knew that they needed it and needed a lot of it.

Once we dumped the large container, we were allowed to return to our cell. A small pile of dried roots and a ceramic jug of water waited for us. I couldn't eat.

I looked up at the balcony, high above our cell. A watcher stared back at me. The alien still wore a protective suit even though we were no longer in an area where snot would create any danger. They had learned quickly that we were willing to try anything to escape. One of our early attempts had involved smuggling snot back to our cells and hurling it at the guards and watchers. We would have succeeded but they just kept sending more troops in to stop us, not caring about the number of fatalities on either side.

This night, there was something different about the watcher. Instead of standing tall, exerting dominance, the creature was hunched over, leaning against the railing. I pointed out the change in demeanor to Naomi.

"I tell you; something has changed. They're acting differently. There's an air of desperation about them."

"How can you tell? They're aliens and they're behind thick masks."

"You remember what I did on the ship, don't you?" Somehow, she managed a slight smile. "They may be aliens but I've observed them enough to get a pretty good read on them."

Who was I to doubt the ship's psychologist? "Well, what do you think it means?"

Naomi shook her head, "I have no idea."

The lights suddenly went out, as they did every night. We each found the pile of rags and leaves that served as our beds. Sleep always came, no matter how hard we fought it or how active our minds wanted to be. Exhaustion has a way of doing that.

When I awoke, I immediately knew something was different. There had been no loud horn blast and there was no brigade of guards waiting by the door.

"Hurry up, we're leaving," announced Naomi.

Whatever grogginess was clinging to my brain let go immediately. "Leaving? Where are the guards?"

"There aren't any. They're gone. I think they're letting us leave." She pointed toward the doorway. I watched as a dozen of my former shipmates raced through the opening.

"Why would they do that? They've kept us for so . . ." I left my question unfinished. Naomi would have no way of knowing. I didn't need to keep asking stupid questions, I needed to leave.

"What if it's some sort of trap?" I asked.

Naomi laughed. "Does it matter?"

She was right. I quickly climbed to my feet and followed Naomi.

We had no belongings. Everything we brought with us had been taken away years ago. Naomi and I were among the final group to leave. For some reason, I have no idea why, I hesitated at the door. I cursed the thought that I might have some sort of nostalgia for this place.

Before I could follow the others, a watcher appeared in the doorway. I waited for a squad of menacing guards to appear. None did; the watcher was alone.

"I waited to speak to the last to leave. May I talk with you?" it asked, in excellent English.

Anger exploded in my gut. They could speak our language but had never thought to try and communicate with us. They had treated us like animals the entire time of our captivity. I swung my fist, connecting solidly against its metal helmet. I'm certain the punch hurt me more than it hurt the alien, but it felt good.

"Please, I need to explain," said the watcher.

"Explain what? Why you attacked us and made us your slaves."

"Yes, I suppose so."

"I don't want to hear anything from you, I just want you to die." I tried to push my way to the door.

"Your wish will be granted shortly. All of my people are about to die."

I should have just left, but a morbid curiosity had taken root. "What do you mean?"

The watcher bowed his head and removed his helmet. The head that was revealed was ghostly pale and completely hairless. Two sunken black eyes stared at me. The creature's mouth was thin and lipless. I did not see any nose or ears. I had seen the aliens without their armor before, but never this close.

"I am so sorry for what we were forced to do to your people. Some of us did not agree with the way you were treated. We argued with our rulers for a very long time. We wanted to negotiate with you once we mastered your language. A mutually agreeable arrangement could have been reached, but our rulers did not agree. They said it was too late, our situation too desperate."

"So, you just stood by and watched while we slaved in your mines for decades. How many of us died or were killed? And you did nothing to stop it." I wanted to lash out again, but something about the watcher's bearing prevented me. The watcher wouldn't have minded being struck. I think it wanted to be punished.

"We had no choice but to force you to work in the mines. You must understand. The material you collected, sorbonite, is deadly to us. We do not have the technology that you do and had to rely on physical labor. Since we were incapable of that labor, you had to fill that role."

The rest of the crew had probably already left the mine by now. I needed to follow. "I don't have time to listen to you. I need to catch up with my people."

"You can join them shortly. If you hear me out, you will be very glad that you did."

"What else do you have to tell me? You enslaved us so you could get sorbonite, or whatever you call it, because you couldn't get it for yourselves."

The watcher continued to stare at me. I realized that he did not have any eyelids. "The reason we needed the sorbonite is that we were being forced to collect it by another race. Many years ago, our planet was invaded by creatures from a different world. They called themselves Corbin. Unlike you, they did not come in peace. They came to vanquish us. The Corbin would have destroyed us had they not discovered that our planet had an abundant supply of sorbonite. We were allowed to live as long as we gather a specific amount of the material by the time they returned."

The watcher extended its hands toward me. "Thousands of my

people died trying to collect the sorbonite. No matter what we tried there was no way we were ever going to be able to collect enough. Then your ship landed. We were desperate. We had to force you to do our labor."

"We could have helped you. We could have used our technology to work the mines."

The watcher bowed his head. "We did not know that at first. By the time we mastered your language, it was too late. You had already been put to work in the mines and we were so far behind our quota that we could not afford to change our strategy."

"And why are you letting us go now? Have we collected enough sorbonite?"

"No, we are far short of the required amount. We have realized that we will never make it. The Corbin are due to return. When they find that we have not succeeded they will punish us. The punishment is extinction. I am sorry. We should have just let you go, but we couldn't work the mines. We needed you."

"Do you honestly think that you are doing us a favor by releasing us now? If the Corbin are coming to destroy you, they're going to destroy us at the same time." I wanted to feel some degree of sorrow for the fact that their entire race was going to be destroyed, but I couldn't. "You're getting what you deserve."

"Yes, we are," replied the watcher, still not displaying any obvious emotion. "But your people will have a chance to escape. Your ship is still on our planet. It has not been harmed. Some of us hoped to use it to escape, but we have not been able to understand your science. I waited here to tell you the location of the ship."

"You mean there's a chance for us to get off this planet before the Corbin get here."

"There should be time." The watcher handed me a map, etched on a plastic-like material, and pointed to two spots. "This is where we are and this is where you will find your ship. It may still function."

I took the map. I didn't know what to say. This didn't make up for all the suffering that we had been forced to endure; all the lives that had been lost.

I turned to leave but felt the watcher's hand on my arm. "I was wondering if, I and my family could come with you. The rest of my people are hiding. It won't work. The Corbin will destroy our world. But, since I have helped you, maybe, you would help me."

I pushed my way past the watcher and headed toward the mine entrance. I never looked back.

WHAT HAS BEGUN

LISA DIAZ MEYER

Think, if you can: of a dark canyon-sized room, harboring rows upon rows of glowing casket-like cabinets; hibernation chambers with living, sleeping humans dreaming in frozen states. In containment, my dreams are nothing out of the ordinary. In them I'm a child back in our old apartment on Earth, where I play with my younger sister and my parents whisper privately with each other. Other than that, we travelers are suspended, preserved, and unchanging.

If my fellow humans were awake right now, they would see the blackness of the universe out the great windows above. The thousands of planets are mere dots. Occasionally, a nebula of innocent colors swarm in sweet storms across a galaxy. Beautiful, powerful, godlike artwork appears through the voluminous window. Then there's darkness, mostly darkness without a sun or moon to dictate the hour. We create our own time, our own days, by what we're accustomed to. There can't be hours or days out here in this void, only immense time in every direction and dimension possible, as far as...forever. Until we can count no more, and still it will go on.

There is a destination, and we are upon it. A twenty-year journey with the help of this craft, this stolen vessel of duration and space. Fellow passengers age only ten years total in two-year cycles, in groups of two hundred people at a time, thanks to these augmented hibernation pods. I have aged seven years although it should have been five. A faulty and overused hibernation booth spit me out like an overcooked piece of meat two years ago. I've lived from age eighteen to twenty outside containment with the remainder of the other two hundred passengers who had finished their hibernation process. None of these passengers are my family or friends, except the captain and First Mate Garren who are also done with their suspended rotation.

I'm standing in this intricate canyon-sized room among the sleeping, almost jealous of their peaceful rest. My last two years have been tumultuous, and I'm glad the universe is having a hard time out there evolving, changing. The universe had damned our sun and our planet, causing The Alien to come and wreak more devastation. Here I stand on *his* ship, all of us survivors, using it to escape. The metals of this ship are strange and have strange smells and sounds. Most of us have adjusted to it, a few have not. The ship provided us with clothes and food from a "fabricator." Of the food, clothes and cleanliness, the food was the best surprise of all. Before embracing the idea of space travel, our people survived on nothing but army rations, cans and powdered goods, vitamin bars and steroids. We are stronger now with this food. I can feel the difference.

It was recently predicted that we were a few days away from landing on our new world. The captain and the High Council chose a non-populated area of the planet. It will take centuries before the planet's natives and our people to eventually find each other. It's very exciting, yet cold tears wet my cheeks as I study the rows and rows of sleeping family and friends. I am standing before my parents' and sister's pods, watching them in their almost lifeless poses. They look blue, but it is only the strange lighting provided by the alien ship. My father is an extremely handsome man. My younger sister, who will now be my older sister but not by much, resembles him. With thick black eyelashes, long black curly hair, and eye color that's a mix of my mother's amber and my father's blue, has the lightest green eyes of anyone I've ever seen. The thought of my father dealing with her many suitors almost makes me smile through my tears. Then I remember that once we're on the new planet, the high council will reinstate the right to arms. Living in such primitive situations, I think it will be a mistake. Men will undoubtedly fight, and some will undoubtedly fight over her when it's more important to come together as a people and not arm ourselves in times of quarrel. But what do I know? I'm only a clone, a word and idea I regard with hatred. Perhaps, had my parents told me, before I heard it from a stranger's angry accusations…but, maybe they never intended me to know. Anyway, two years ago, the scenario went down in this very room…

The captain, Ernie Rutch, was setting me up for my last stint in hibernation. I was eighteen, aging only five years in twenty. The intention was for me not to age past that before we landed. I was looking down at Ernie as he punched buttons on the panel at my side, and I blurted out because it's in my nature to speak my mind, "You have nice blue eyes."

Ernie blushed. Being of fair skin, it was hard not to see how pink he turned. He put his head back down so I couldn't see him, but the smile in his voice was still audible when he said, "I do? Well, thank you, Sylle."

But I wasn't done teasing him, "You look like a pirate."

"A pirate!" He laughed and stood to set the straps about my shoulders. "What exactly is that?"

I laughed back. "I'm not very sure. But when I was younger, Mr. Harris, the schoolteacher had an old counting book that featured a pirate character, a captain of a boat. Your hair color and facial hair are the same." Blond but slightly darker.

He was smiling and continued to blush. He began to speak when there was a sudden outburst behind him. A man, another passenger from Earth, had come upon my family, shouting about clones, and pointing at me. He said I was inhuman. He said I didn't count. He said that I was a soulless experiment that wasn't worthy of the extra five years in suspended animation. That I was taking the place of someone more deserving and for that, I should be shot dead.

Ernie's light blue eyes locked with mine, and he shut the door starting my hibernation process. The last thing I saw was my father and Ernie trying to calm the irate intruder. The gasses filled the container and I fell asleep with shouts that never made it to my lips.

Three years later, just after my family went in for their last process, my pod door opened. My sleep and hibernation wore off. The pod malfunctioned, and there wasn't the usual slow detox. I blindly unfastened myself and landed on my knees. The last of the water and hibernation fluid I'd breathed in came up in a clear rush instead of being absorbed into my intestinal tract as it would have during a normal five-year containment/detox mode. What had happened? Where was everyone? Usually, someone from my family was present to greet me. But I was alone in the giant, cavernous hibernation room. Well, not completely alone. Two hundred other passengers were asleep in their pods unaware of my plight. Blue lights lit them from inside. Subconsciously, I knew they all were asleep, but they looked monstrous. From blue face to blue face, I was surrounded by lifeless looking people. I started screaming. Between the disorientation and the stillness of the alien room, I felt as if I'd never stop. Instead, I passed out. Fear and insufficient detox had done me in.

Soon after, I regained consciousness as the captain gave orders to someone nearby. I attempted to move, but I was thoroughly weakened by what that chamber had done to me.

"It's OK, Sylle. I'm bringing you to Dr. Rose. She'll fix ya right up," Ernie assured. I didn't doubt him. Ernest Rutch had been our captain and in charge of our escape since stepping aboard. I let myself pass out again without a struggle.

I was sick for only a few days, laid up in the infirmary. Ernie came by whenever possible. I was alone; my family was still locked in the sleep chambers. Ernie wanted to awaken one or both of my parents, knowing one would change places with me and age the two years instead of me. I told him no. My parents weren't getting any younger, and what was the big deal if I aged two years? I'd only be twenty. It took a bit of arguing; Ernie wasn't easily swayed. Finally, I claimed my right as an adult and said I was never getting into another hibernation booth again after being so sick. To the latter, he forfeited his argument.

"All right," he softened. His pale blue eyes were searching my face as if he was trying to read my mind but couldn't.

"I have questions…"

"I figured." He smiled.

"Did someone sabotage my hibernation booth?" I know it sounded paranoid, but what about the argument between that strange man and my father as I went under? Again odd.

"No, I checked into it. According to the surveillance records it was just a fluke, a malfunction of the pod. I know everything about this ship, and it's rare that something should break down. To us, all this alien technology is brand new, but it isn't. It's very old."

I nodded. "It's all right. I never liked being under anyway."

"Five years at a time is rough. I won't make you go back."

I nodded again. I wanted to ask him why my hibernation regimen was stricter than anyone else's. Everyone was in containment two years in and then two years out, but mine was five years in and five years out. But I stopped myself from asking. If my own family hadn't told me, I could not ask the captain about it. I would take it upon myself to figure it out.

Dr. Rose soon released me, and I headed for our family's quarters. The four of us lived in one, and my grandparents bunked in another nearby. They were all unoccupied now, so I had a bit of privacy. The two hundred people from this section of the ship were in containment. I took lonely jogs up and down the empty corridors. The echoes sounded sensationally ominous.

Finally, I got up the nerve to visit the alien library. It would tell me what I wanted to know about human clones, without human concerns. I didn't bother with the books that could be translated easily into any language the aliens had knowledge of. Instead I chose a private library booth. It had a seat and a floating screen, it spoke, and it saved information. It also offered privacy, as there were some people out of hibernation mulling around. I asked my question, never thinking of its consequences or how I'd feel afterward.

"Tell me," I ordered it, "everything about Earth's human clones."

And it did. Perhaps I could've used some human concern, after all, because I didn't like what I heard. S. Mitchell (that would be me, the only living specimen) was a science experiment, like any plant or fungus. So, the strange passenger three years ago had been right. I wasn't human; I was a copy, a healthy duplicate of my mother. My dad was not my dad. My sister was not my sister. I was my mother's imitation. I was not my own person, not Sylle Mitchell. And lastly, I learned about the shortened life span, the torturous five-year hibernation stints, the reason my family tried to keep me younger. If not harvested in time, by forty, my organs would age and deteriorate quicker because I was just a rushed, botched, and unperfected lab experiment.

The wave of self-pity I felt was devastating. I let myself drown in it. They weren't my feelings anyway. There was no *me*. Sylle Mitchell was a lie, and Sylle Mitchell was alone, a cancer-immune clone with a shortened life span and the only one in humanity created like this. Cold, calculated, and soulless. I didn't leave my quarters for days. I couldn't eat. I lay in the dark waiting to wither away, no matter how long it took or how painful.

I'm not sure how many days passed before I was rescued again by the captain. He'd broken the entry code to my quarters and took me once again to the sick bay. Once I was strong enough, Ernie, who had been my thrice-a-day visitor, literally spoon-fed me all my meals. He asks me what in the hell I thought I was doing.

My answer was a shrug. I hated his disappointment, but I detested the idea that I was a clone even more. "You're just worried because as the captain, you are responsible for four hundred lives." I said harshly.

"But, Sylle," Ernie admitted, "if something does happen to you, I couldn't live with myself. When it comes to you, there's more to it."

"Explain," I challenged him.

He shook his head. Ernie was in his early thirties. He walked and talked with great authority. He is just under six feet tall and on the thinner side of an average build. I knew he was supposed to be a genius or something, that's why the alien had abducted him in the first place. But I also just realized that Ernie had always treated me differently. Now I knew why. I was a clone, not a real human.

"No. You're going to tell me why you'd starve yourself."

"I'm not who I thought I was. I figured it was best to die than to deteriorate internally, maybe even painfully, before I hit forty. I understand why I had to go into hibernation longer... to keep me from aging. I'm a clone, a copy of someone who already exists."

Ernie was quiet through my tirade. I don't think he expected any of that, and for a few moments he looked sincerely heartbroken. I hadn't noticed that he gently held my hand until he brought our intertwined fingers into view.

"We have a lot in common. Except... you have people who love you and accept you." He stopped abruptly, allowing it to sink in. We both knew that he had neither family nor friends. Then he explained that he was moving my quarters nearer to his. He wanted me away from the empty, lonely portion of the ship while the two hundred or so people that usually occupied those corridors were in hibernation mode. I agreed to it. It was excruciatingly lonely. The design and layout of the alien ship had a sorrowful and creepy aspect to both human and clone.

Once there, I jogged around the new corridors daily. No one got in the way; the other two-hundred passengers should've been exercising more themselves. I usually wore a white T-shirt and exercise pants, with my hair up in a big red ponytail. I was hard to miss. When I told Ernie, I wanted to learn how to fight, I received the biggest smile.

"I'll find you a teacher," he complied.

"Well, what about you? Can't you teach me?"

"I'm not much of a fighter," he said, "but you go ahead and learn."

So, he set me up with a sparring partner, who was very good and very fast. We fought with heavily padded weapons and met twice a week, if not more, depending on his availability. Sometimes Ernie came to watch but never participated. Then he and I would head back to our rooms to meet up for his dinner break.

I asked during one of our evening meals. "I know I'm supposed to know you my whole life—?"

"We do," he interrupted, "almost. I was just a kid when I met your parents, you were barely two years old. I apprenticed in your mother and father's blacksmith shop."

"Then you were gone, with the alien, on this ship." Funny, once he was back on Earth, he visited my parents, but I barely paid him any mind. I was ten years old then, too busy getting braces and too busy with friends like the Wynn brothers and the Michaelson girls. Then there was the miserable and infamous Duma Harris murder trial, and later we were brought on board in shifts to get the hang of life on this space vessel. That alone took three long years. By then my braces were gone and I was thirteen. "May I ask … after your abduction how did you get the alien to come back to our planet?"

Ernie stopped eating and said seriously, "Once he trusted me, I tricked him. He would need hibernation frequently. I made sure he didn't wake up and I set a course back to Earth. I wanted to kill him then but he was too strong. It just wasn't time—"

"He woke up though," I interrupted.

"Yes."

His way of not being very talkative had become common. I think it had to do with what the alien did to him or taught him.

"Sylle? After your sparring lessons, would you like to join me on a little excursion? Show you something of the alien's life?"

With excitement I agreed. I could barely sleep that night wondering what it would be like. Then there was my joy at being alone with the captain, with Ernie, and having him to myself for at least a little while.

The excursion turned out to be extraordinary. One would think it extraordinary enough to board an alien ship, but no, the excursion through this wondrous ship with the captain and learning about the alien were eye opening. The entirety of the vessel was disturbing to humans with its unreadable hieroglyphics and grim patterns displayed everywhere. Its design to make the alien comfortable made us feel threatened. It was nothing like our culture on Earth. All I knew environmentally was a blacksmith shop on a run-down, half-built Outpost. This advanced alien civilization felt cold and foreign, disagreeable. Whenever the ship's oppressive and repugnant appearance became overwhelming, I'd vehemently remind myself that it was just a transport vessel, a way to get to a promising new planet.

Ernie was taking me to a part of the ship I'd never been to, way below the decks we normally lived on. It was darker there, the air dense and humid. I had to breathe in deeply. I trusted Ernie to lead me to significant curiosities. Finally, a set of double doors blocked our way. I couldn't tell if they were made of stone, wood, or something else, but the etchings were incredibly designed, even more intricate than any of the hieroglyphs scattered around the ship.

"It's beautiful," I blurted out.

"It's an ancient lore of dedication. And yes, it is beautiful," he agreed. "You ready?" He soundlessly pushed the two doors inward. I followed him respectfully as he walked in.

The room's walls were covered with mostly green plant life, the same kind I'd learned about in the alien library when I was out of hibernation.

"Here is some blue moss and lichen. There, some clinging vine and ivy-like plants." Ernie pointed out what grew in the corners. "The stone here is from the alien's planet."

Ernie smiled. "It's a form of gold. Our planet had its own version in abundance. But that was before the first bombings, before you and I were born."

I didn't know what to make of this room. The alien was dead, yet I felt as though I had invaded its privacy. I got the feeling Ernie had never shared this place with anyone else.

"You see that stand? The black column? It acts like a hologram, a three-D projection. It doesn't follow my voice command, though. Only the aliens. Watch," he said to me and pointed a wand remote at it. Above the stand a picture appeared, moving and three-dimensional as he'd said. The figure in the picture was clearly a woman. This glowing ethereal creature surrounded by total blackness floated up and down in front of me.

"This is a hologram of the alien's mate. She will wait forever for his return home. If she were really here, she would be over seven feet tall." Ernie adjusted the wand, and the hovering hologram became life size. Now the feminine creature almost took up the entirety of the room with long, drifting, phosphorescent hair and tendrils floating in the blackness. Her glowing veined wings beat slowly. They upheld her, suspended her in the viscous fluid so her tiny feet never met the ground. "The alien females live submerged in their vast oceans far below the surface. On their planet, the oceans are so pitch black that over time the aquatic female evolved to produce her own light."

She was slender yet curvy, and her face pinched outward like a pixie. Her skin sparkled blue and purple shades making her even more luxe. If I dared turn away, I might miss a nuance I hadn't noticed yet. She constantly moved and changed.

"She is lovely," I said. "Did he love her?"

Ernie laughed. "Oh yeah. The alien, my alien abductor, did, very much. He spoke of her often." Ernie paused with a grit to his teeth. "He was angry that I was capable of turning the ship around, that I'd tricked him. He wanted me dead. My only course was to kill him, but he needed to be weaker for me to do it. It had to be the perfect moment. Except Duma Harris was on guard nearby, and the alien mortally wounded him. Mentally, there was nothing left of Duma; his brain died quickly. At that point, I had to kill Duma, as well as the alien." He shut the hologram down.

"I'm sorry," I whispered. "I liked Duma Harris very much. We all did. They said you two were childhood friends."

"We were," he concurred.

We left the lichen-clad room and ancient drawings behind us.

"I'm sorry," I said again.

He'd openly confessed to killing the old schoolteacher's son, Officer Duma Harris, his once best friend, and all I could offer him was a sorry. Genius Ernie Rutch, our Captain, led a weird life. Even though he was saving us, even being around Earth people now, he lived in solitude. In some way, I was going to be the same with my clone identity known. Soon everyone would know it, and I'd be shunned. I held Ernie's hand; for some reason, I was afraid for us both.

~

Days later, the vision of the alien female still stuck in my thoughts. Her image both frightened and delighted me. To me, she was unique and perfect, two things I was not. Then there was the history and timeline that I didn't want to think about concerning the Duma Harris murder. Who had done what to whom was unfortunate collateral damage decades ago and was now of no consequence.

Ernie knocked, bringing in our dinner. I'd been stargazing, as usual, out the portal-sized window in my apartment. It was common that he took his dinner breaks with me, and when he could, he'd come to watch my sparring lessons.

"I have questions tonight," I told him while we ate.

"Have you?" he joked, as I always had questions.

"Yes." I laughed. "And I know you only get an hour break before Garren comes looking for you, so I'll try and be quick."

He smiled. "OK, ask."

"Do you think of me as Sylle or a replica of my mother?"

"You're going to be serious tonight, I see."

"Yes. Very."

He thought only a moment and said, "You, Sylle Mitchell, are not like your mother. Of course, you look like her twenty years younger, except that you wear your hair differently. Clone or not, you are not the same person. Your mother's life was very hard, while you were given every chance to be yourself. Your childhood was a happy one. You were raised so differently that although you have her exact chromosomes and genes, you are not the same in the least. You, Sylle, are all I see when I look at you."

Ernie's words stunned me. To my ears, they were magical. I loved them. I loved that he spoke them to me. Whispered words started to fall out of my mouth.

"Ernie, I think—"

"I might as well admit this, Sylle. I love you. Our age difference, though, might present a..."

"I don't care about ages, Ernie. I love you." It felt wonderful to say and admit the words out loud, so I said them again. "I love you."

When we were apart, I couldn't wait to see him. And when we were together, I never wanted our moments to end. And as for ages, I was eighteen. I'd be older had they let me age normally. It didn't matter; with our admissions tonight, my life had just begun.

During the next two years, up until I was twenty, my life was filled with nothing but romance and love. We couldn't keep our hands off each other. Playful, serious, passionate. We were silly and we were intense in the most beautiful of comparisons. He was considerate and consuming all at once. We spent all our time together. He now sparred with me and let me kick his ass. He tried to jog around the empty corridors with me. I would laugh and go back for him when he gave up, leaning over and gasping for air. We played human card games or alien dice games and laughed and joked for hours. We held hands, always touching. I trimmed his pirate goatee and spiked his blond pirate hair. I was Sylle and he was Ernest. Me, the clone that the hero loved and he, the hero this clone wanted for the rest of her short life. I pledged, he would know nothing but my love, safety, and respect, and I would know his.

Or so I thought. A few days before we were to enter the new planet's atmosphere, Ernie didn't return to our room at night. Positive he and First Mate Garren were busy, I let it be. The next night it was the same. I went searching for him, the man with whom I was going to conquer a new world. The first time I went to the bridge Garren was there, but not Ernie.

"Where's the captain?" I asked him.

"He went on break, Miss Mitchell."

Break? I thought with confusion. I hurried back to our quarters to see if he was there, but he wasn't. He was intentionally avoiding me. Why? Why would Ernie do that, especially now that we were almost *home*? Out of all the emotions coursing inside me—sadness, anger, confusion, —confusion was at the top of the list.

The second time I headed for the bridge both Garren and the captain were there and occupied. Something on the screen had their complete attention. I didn't care. I was getting my questions answered.

Ernie watched me enter with red-rimmed eyes beneath his dark blond lashes. He looked tired, and suddenly it occurred to me I might not want to hear what he was thinking. So instead of anger, my voice was full of fear.

"I want to know what's going on."

"Yes. We have to talk, Sylle."

"Talk?" I asked.

I wanted to scream at him, not talk. I wanted to hold him, not talk. What was there to discuss?

"Yes, talk."

I suddenly felt stupid, small... heartbroken. I turned and left, and once I felt I was in safe enough distance, I jogged quickly back to our quarters. In the morning, I realized I didn't want to *talk*, so I took whatever was mine from the captain's rooms and brought them back to my family's quarters on the empty side of the ship, back where I was two years ago when that miserable hibernation chamber broke down on me. Did those two years mean anything? Had they even happened? Could I have imagined it on this damned alien ship?

They would all be coming out of the hibernation booths today. Their slow detox process would be mild, unlike the last one I was subjected to two years ago. The last two hundred people would finally awaken. Among them, my family, and friends. And I'd be there to greet them, heartbroken and teary-eyed but there, nonetheless. I stood before the chambers, the enormous window above still displaying the quiet, endless black sky and the blue lights in each of the pods still illuminating all those sleeping faces. It was an unforgiving light. No one looked good in it.

Eventually I heard footsteps. Someone else was walking through the rows. It was Ernie. He'd found me. With the new planet coming into view, it would be easy to guess where I might be. Right with the family and friends I knew on Earth.

"I have something I need to explain."

"Don't bother. I don't want to hear it." I didn't look at him. I really didn't want to hear it.

"The last few days I needed to show Garren the procedure as we enter the atmosphere because… I would not be on the bridge. I wanted to be here with you."

I still didn't respond.

"Sylle, I should've told you sooner. Ugh, this is so difficult to say."

My silence didn't deter him, and he continued.

"When we land and all is well with the new community and its location, I must leave our group. I've been banished. The Duma Harris murder trial…the outcome. I killed Duma; I pled guilty. Keeping me jailed only wastes resources. And the council won't sentence me because I've brought everyone safely to the new planet. But they also don't want to see me walking around free. They'll all be getting their weapons back…"

I wanted to glance up at him, but I kept my teary eyes on my hibernating parents. "They know you had to kill Duma Harris. You said the alien rendered him brain dead."

"Yes, but his older brother is on the High Council, and he's not so forgiving." Ernie waved his hands in a helpless gesture. "He blames me for all of it. And he's right. Duma was killed."

I sighed, feeling beaten.

"The best solution was that I be banished from the new settlement."

"Then take me with you," I pressed.

"I can't, Sylle. It's not your punishment. You have a great family. I won't separate you from them. There will be other, worthier young men"—he paused momentarily to swallow—"like Marcus Wynn."

"Wait, so you want me to be with Marcus Wynn?" I asked in confusion.

"No." He raised his voice slightly. "I do not *want* that! But you cannot come with me, and I can't stay with the group. I have to leave."

My tears blurred as a bright light flashed through the giant window beyond the rows of pods. We'd entered the atmosphere of our new planet. The twenty years of travel was coming to an end. The suspended two hundred would awake, my family would swarm me… and Ernie would be gone from my life.

"What is my future, Ernie?" I whispered.

"I can't see your future, Sylle. You know that," he whispered, too.

"No, but what do you want for your own? Am I in it?"

We finally looked at each other. His answer took forever, *my* forever in a matter of seconds.

"Yes."

We held each other. Nothing mattered while the dead black space beyond turned ever bluer and brighter. The metal and rock sleep chambers surrounding us started their countdown.

"Then why are you trying to stop it?" I implored.

"I won't. I won't," he sighed. "I'll figure something out, I promise. We won't be separated." Ernie whispered undeniable apologies in my ears, and I cried tears of relief while my heavy heart mended inside my chest.

I'd fight the banishment and petition the High Council until they could no longer stand the sight of me. Ernie had rescued us from our rotting planet and dying sun. Ernie, who'd been abducted and tortured, had delivered us to a new world giving us all a second chance. How could we start society anew with such hypocrisy? We tightly held hands and watched as the hibernation pod lights turned off and my family gradually started coming to life. Their detox cycle began just as we descended into the new planet's peaceful daylight clouds.

DIVE INTO THE BLUE INFERNO

J.R. RUSTRIAN

The rickety hovercar shuddered slightly as it sat idle in the bumper-to-bumper traffic. The glass encased tube that was the highway was clogged from that morning's rush hour and showed no signs of easing. Up ahead, a local sheriff, sporting dark sunglasses, a khaki shirt, pants, and a terribly worn, wide brimmed hat, poked his head into each hovercar, and received a small white envelope for his trouble. From his vantage point, Dominic Dominguez and Julio Obregon could see the sheriff moving at a leisurely pace, going through his daily rounds of extortion.

"Don't say a word," said Andrew, their driver, weather scientist and local guide, "He'll leave once I pay him off."

"He's not going to recognize Dom, is he?" asked Julio, craning his neck to look through the windshield.

"Pray that he doesn't watch television."

The three watched as the sheriff, with not an ounce of trepidation, poked his head into their hovercar.

"Duties?" he asked in a gruff voice with a hint of a foreign accent.

Andrew reached into the middle console, pulled out a small envelope stuffed full of Neptunian currency, and handed it to the cop. The sheriff smiled as he eagerly grabbed the envelope and then briefly turned his attention to Dom. He looked back at the sheriff and confidently smiled. The sheriff nodded, looked towards the street, and returned several of the crisp dollar bills to Andrew.

"Dangerous Dom Dominguez? Big fan, sir. Followed your stuff for years. I saw that Ganymede jump you made. Can't believe you're still alive," he said with a massive grin on his face. Ahead of them, the cars began to move down the street. The sheriff tipped his hat and walked past them to the next row of cars.

"Are you kidding me?" said an exasperated Andrew as he accelerated the car "I don't think I've ever seen that happen before here."

Dom leaned back and smirked, "What can I say? Nereid Station loves me."

The hovercar veered right and continued onto a smaller roadway heading away from the main streets of Nereid Station, the main trading post serving the outer planets which floated ominously in the thin clouds surrounding Neptune. Despite the imaginable beauty of the blue hue of the planet, Nereid Station was as rustic as rustic could get out among the gas giants; and that was being generous to a former mining colony.

From outside, Nereid Station looked like any other glass and titanium covered colony that might float around their home planet. It had a central economic hub surrounded by several, smaller neighborhoods where the residents of the station spent their days either breaking their backs hard at work or living off that labor in luxury. Either way, there were ways of making money there and it was up to each person to find out how, laws be damned.

With the massive amount of money flowing through Nereid Station, it was inevitable that it was going to turn into a cesspool. The sheriff was just one of the many ways that Nereid Station could greet you, along with junkies, lowlifes, and criminals of every sort. All of this suited Dom just fine; the more they were concerned with themselves, the less they would be concerned with him.

"How far away is this satellite?" asked Julio, writing several things down on his tablet.

"Only about half an hour. The staff is gone for a few hours and they left me in charge. You've got that big of a window to get it done."

"That's all we're going to need, Andy, my boy. Have you checked the weather conditions?" asked Dom, eagerly looking outside the front of the hovercar for any sign of the satellite.

"I did before I left. Cloud conditions are good and wind speeds are at a minimum, but I'm a little afraid of the ice levels."

"Ha, that's just wonderful. Step on it, we have a schedule to keep."

There was something about this Andrew kid that he liked, thought Dom. A real go-getter. A nerd, sure, but able to get things done. He could hear it in his voice the moment Julio contacted him about coming to Neptune. It took several tries to find the right person to convince. Everyone else either had no idea who Dom was or were too responsible to let some crazy, aging stratojumper come and potentially cause unnecessary headaches.

Andrew was the type who yearned for more excitement, more action, more out of life. He was easy to entice into bending several of Nereid Station's already lax laws in order to plan Dom's next big jump. If all went well, Andrew would go down in history. It also helped that Dom promised him a hefty sum from the licensing deals of the eventual recordings.

The hovercar came to the end of the physical road. At the rear of the car, rocket jets ignited, jolting the three forward and sending them up and out into the methane and hydrogen which made up Neptune's upper atmosphere. They climbed higher towards the edge of space, leaving behind the thin, white clouds and towards the blanket of stars. Dom could feel his heart beat faster. The exhilaration was nearly overwhelming.

He turned to his left and spied Julio munching on a pack of peanuts and wiping his hands on his pants. Julio was sloppy by nature, but not when it came to his ability to make things happen. There was a subtle charm that he possessed which contrasted with the bombast that Dom threw around. Julio's ability to get a great shot out of any of his antics was also an invaluable asset.

Dom smirked and cracked his knuckles. It was exactly his qualities that made him fall in love with Julio all those years ago. From the most extremes of bone-breaking pain to the greatest of joys, Julio was always there for him. Amazingly enough, it was Julio who worked up the courage to admit it to him, not the daredevil in the spacesuits.

"I have to say, I'm still really nervous about you making this jump," said Andrew, looking at the two using the rear-view mirror.

"Relax, Andy. I've made two Meteor Drops before," answered Dom.

"Two *attempted* Meteor Drops," interjected Julio.

"Yes, but I still survived."

Julio scoffed, "Barely."

"I walked out of there with all my limbs intact."

"After hours of surgery."

Dom rolled his eyes and looked ahead as they lurched over a cloud-bank, rattling the rickety hovercar. Julio wasn't wrong. His partner and manager had been there since the beginning, recording his stunts, promoting his work, and patching up each and every injury. They met one day in the seventh grade, after Julio jumped off the high dive to show off for his fellow classmates. Dom immediately climbed to the top of the roof of Julio's house and jumped into the pool, breaking his pinky and winning the admiration of not only his friends but Julio as well.

In the distance, an orange beacon flashed in three second intervals. The satellite was tiny in comparison to other, more modern ones; no more than two football fields in length and shaped like a top. The sharp bottom of the satellite pointed towards the planet, sending a constant stream of data down through the thick atmosphere. It was almost like an arrow pointing towards your next destination.

They were almost there. Dom looked over at Julio like he had many times over their thirty years together sharing a life and planning increasingly suicidal jumps. He often wondered how Julio could stay with somebody so out of their mind. Julio was always so cautious in his daily life. Hell, he would never even chance a red light. Dom winced at the mere thought of Julio injuring himself on a stunt. He must be with me for my money, Dom joked to himself.

"Hey, so uh, you never told me exactly how you're going to attempt this Meteor Drop. Hell, I don't even think I really get what exactly a Meteor Drop is supposed to be," said Andrew.

"Well…" started Julio "You've seen Dom's dive over the cryovolcanoes of Ganymede, right?"

"Yeah, I've seen it."

"It's nothing like that at all. It's the fastest, scariest, wildest thing any person can do in the entire solar system."

"I still don't follow."

Julio leaned against the car door. "You go to a set height, avail yourself of all means of propulsion, and just jump straight down with nothing with gravity cradling your body. Hopefully, you'll hit terminal velocity before your body starts to burn up from re-entry."

As they approached Nereid Satellite #5, they could see the weather, icy metal sides of the aging science station. The hovercar decelerated for its landing inside the tiny hangar. Inside, Dom and Julio could see two other hovercars; one stripped for parts the other with the former mining company's logo on its side.

"I'll put it this way, Andy-man," said Dom, "Every planet in the solar system has its own Meteor Drop. The first was obviously Earth's. Then we got the rest of the inner planets out of the way. Easy, since they got solid surfaces, but where it gets really tricky is when you get out here with the gas giants. No solid surfaces, right? You've gotta be extra careful or else you'll get yourself crushed."

"Don't forget that it's also completely illegal to attempt any Meteor Drops," added Julio.

"Yikes. I'm sorry I even asked." said Andrew, pulling the car into the hangar "but it shouldn't be too bad this time around right? Shorter jump, yeah? I have a safe house set up on Nereid Station so you can lay low if any local authorities see you coming in," said Andrew, leaning forward to get a better view for his landing.

"Yeah…about that. We aren't doing Nereid Station," said Dom with a grin on his face.

Andrew looked up at the rear-view mirror. "What are you talking about?"

"Andy, have you ever heard of the Blue Inferno?"

The car skidded as it landed inside the hangar. Andrew slammed on the brakes, bouncing off the stripped hovercar and nearly smashing into a set of concrete stairs. Dom smiled massively, trying to remove

Julio's powerful grip off his arm. He leaned forward and patted a shocked Andrew on the shoulder.

"An-dy! That was awesome, man!"

"Are you out of your goddamn mind?" screamed Andrew, standing in front of weather projections and other scientific data. "They're going to arrest all of us and then they're going to kick my ass out of science. Not Neptune, not Nereid, not the outer planets. Out of science! You get me?"

Dom and Julio watched as Andrew raved and ranted in front of them. He shoved a chair and then slapped pen and pencils off his own desk. A few minutes later, in the middle of his rant, he picked them up and placed them back on his desk.

Dom wasn't particularly paying attention. His gaze frequently went up to the atomic clock that was set up across the western wall. The minutes were quickly counting down, giving him less and less time to get ready for the drop. He tapped his legs, slightly nervous but excited.

"I get that I lied to you, Andy..." said Dom.

"My name is Andrew!" screamed Andrew. Dom put his hands up in defense.

"Fine. Andrew. I knew you were never going to approve of us coming to the satellite if I told you that I wanted to take on the Blue Inferno, so I had to stretch the truth a little."

Andrew looked at Dom and Julio and shook his head. "Get out. Just get out. I don't wanna see you two again."

"We can't, genius. You drove us here," said Julio.

"Then take my keys. Just go. I'm not having anything to do with this anymore." Andrew stomped off to his computer console and turned back to the two. Dom's heart skipped a beat. He was minutes away from capturing the most renowned record in the solar system. Every moment he wasted was more time for other stratojumpers to make their mark and he wasn't getting any younger. Dom looked over at Julio and spied the ever-present cautiousness that was on his face. How they remained together he could never figure out.

"Maybe he's right, Dom. You're probably in over your head here," said Julio, crossing his arms.

"What? Are you crazy? No, just wait." Dom slowly walked over to Andrew's console and sat down on his desk.

"I've heard the Blue Inferno is one of the wildest, windiest, iciest places in all of the solar system, but it's pretty this time of year," said Dom, checking his nails.

"Not one of, Dom. THE most," said Andrew.

"Yeah? How so?"

"Where to start? Three hundred mile per hour winds, massive chunks of icy methane, incredibly dangerous lightning storms, not to mention the crushing pressure if you go deep enough. We barely know enough about it as it is."

"Yeah, you're right. Suppose sending a small probe into that maelstrom, one that could collect all sorts of data. One who would be *very* eager to go and one you didn't have to pay for."

Andrew's ears perked up. He swiveled in his chair and looked at Dom. Their mutual need for recognition connected for an instant. Andrew was hungry to prove himself but shared a frustrating cautiousness with Julio. Andrew was some sort of mixture of himself and his friend, like a weird son abandoned on some rusty satellite orbiting Neptune.

"Imagine being the first to discover and analyze that data, Andrew. Lots of fame, hm? Beats being stuck in here, doesn't it?"

Andrew sneered, looked around the room, then to his console and then to the two. "Suppose I said yes. We'd probably have to contact someone at Marina Mining Station to make sure their beacon is on."

"Yes!" yelled Dom, "I knew I liked you for a reason. Let's get started."

An hour later, Dom fiddled with his helmet before the pressurization procedure initiated. Julio clipped the last of his boots to the rest of his titanium-nylon weaved suit. Across the glass faceplate, numbers, letters, and other scientific terms flashed across Dom's face. He ignored it, rather more content to work on the map, altitude, and air jet systems.

"I'm getting a bad feeling about this, Dom," said Julio, looking outside a massive viewport located at the bottom of the satellite; the part where Dom planned to jump out of.

"You say that all the time, buddy," said Dom. "Initiate pressurization."

"Sure, I do, but only because I'm serious about it. This isn't like anything you've jumped before."

"I've jumped Venus before."

"Easy. All you had to do was to make sure your suit didn't melt. It was a seven-minute fall before Jon Marius broke the record."

Dom sighed loudly. He didn't want to be reminded about Jon Marius or any other stratojumper. He was pushing fifty and just about every one of his records were being broken by younger, highly driven jumpers. They were plunging headlong into sub-zero oceans of methane or orbiting rogue comets in under sixteen hours. He began to feel the sting of being obsolete.

"Which is it?" said Julio, snapping him out of his thoughts. "Being first or being highest?"

Dom sniffed, cracked his knuckles, and stood next to the airlock. "Both."

Julio smirked and patted him on the back. "I'd try to talk you out of it, but we both know that's useless. Good luck, buddy."

Julio stepped out of the room and closed the heavy steel door behind him. Dom opened the airlock and stepped inside. The room depressurized, leaving Dom at the mercy of the lethal Neptunian atmosphere. He stepped outside and switched on his gravity boots. They clunked heavily among the metal alloy hull of the satellite as he walked to the jump off point.

"Dom? It's Andrew. Can you hear me?" Dom heard Andrew's mousey voice come through the comms.

"I hear you, my man."

"I did a final scan of the Inferno. Clouds are at a minimum, but ice conditions are a little bad. Are you sure you wanna go through with this?"

"Records are made to be broken, Andy. Never forget that." Dom slowly walked down to the lowest point of Nereid Station. He stared down into the Blue Inferno, raging and churning like a whirlpool. It welcomed him into its heart with a hearty laugh, knowing and craving just what it can do anybody foolish enough to step inside. For a moment, Dom felt hesitation. "Julio, make sure the cameras are set on me and you're recording the descent. This means nothing if we don't have proof."

"Cameras are all set, buddy. Your beacon is transmitting loud and clear."

"Are you sure, Julio?" Dom asked sternly, his eyes transfixed on the Inferno, "Promise me that they're recording."

"Hey, Dom, relax. I've got you, okay? Now promise that you're going to follow all my advice."

Dom chuckled, "I promise. I'll see you top side in a few hours. Count me down, guys." He bent his knees and readied to push off the side of the satellite. The suit's internal supercomputer calculated the last of the waypoints to guide him down to Marina Station. Through the helmet's speakers, he heard his partners' voices count down.

Three...

Dom breathed heavily. He could feel the sweat between his fingers.

Two...

He bent his knees and winced as he felt the left one crack.

One!

Dom deactivated the gravity boots and forcefully pushed off the side of the satellite, sending him flying like a bullet through the thin, blue clouds of Neptune. The blackness of space overhead rapidly disappeared into the horizon, giving way to an azure ocean of gas. Tiny bits of methane ice bounced off the suit, making a sound which resembled a farm tractor driving over a road of loose gravel.

Immediately, Dom was tossed side to side by the thick clouds, making it difficult to keep his bearings. The navigation inside his face-plate tumbled every which way. A strong burst of wind tossed him and spun him head over heels. He struggled to correct himself and orient his head downwards.

"Dom, how's it going?" Julio's voice came over the comm.

"I'm tumbling, Julio, give me a sec."

Dom scrambled to push a button on his left arm, deploying the drag flaps that covered his metallic suit. The flaps slowed his descent and, along with the air jets, finally corrected his posture, falling belly first into the icy abyss.

"Okay, we're good, Julio. Andrew, how are we looking?" Dom yelled over the rushing wind.

"Icy, like I said. Just follow the navigation, Dom."

Dom's eyes shifted towards the navigation on his faceplate. He wasn't even at one-fourth the distance towards Marina Station and already he was off course, thanks to the tumble right after the drop. He was approaching terminal velocity and struggling to see anything other than pure azure blankness.

"Can't see shit out here guys," yelled Dom.

"It's all clouds and ice from here to the station, buddy," Julio said back.

"Doesn't even look like clouds. Looks like somebody splashed paint onto my faceplate."

"It's a blueout," said Andrew, "Everything blends together. Just stick to your waypoints and you'll be fine."

A strong blast rattled Dom. Right on cue, he smashed past the sound barrier, becoming the first human to go supersonic without a spaceship on Neptune. The turbulence increased dramatically, rattling Dom side by side as if he were in the middle of a massive crowd struggling to find an exit. The waypoints on his navigation glowed red, signaling that he needed to correct his course immediately.

Suddenly, a massive crack of thunder exploded near Dom, scrambling his faceplate into a blizzard of interference. Ice spread across his suit, causing him to fall faster and harder. A gigantic thunderstorm enveloped him. Massive streaks of lightning cracked in every direction, some nearly blinding him.

"Andrew, you son of a bitch, you said it was going to be clear!" yelled Dom, trying to clear some of the ice on his visor.

"Weather report said it was clear. I don't even know where it came from!"

"When I get back, I'm going to strangle you, you hear me?"

"Ye-...but th-..can-...-tch it, okay?" Bits and pieces of human speech dissolved into static. Nereid Station was completely cut off.

"Hello? Anybody? Hello?" Dom cried in vain. A tingle crawled up his spine. He suddenly felt alone, miles away from anybody else. He continued to plunge into the Inferno, dodging massive bolts of lightning and fighting off the buildup of ice on his suit.

Ahead, the flashes of lightning blocked out a looming black mass. Dom struggled to see what exactly it was. The ice made it supremely difficult to see anything other than blue darkness. Then, a cold sensation clicked in his head. Inside his helmet, an alarm went off.

He pressed on his air jets and attempted to swerve to his right but was too late to miss the gargantuan piece of ice and rock ahead of him. Dom slid across several meters of icy debris along his left shoulder. A piece of frozen methane knocked his helmet before he fell off the edge and back into the blue unknown.

Dom shook his head. The massive pain in his shoulder signaled the familiar sensation of it being dislocated from its joint. Even more concerning, the top right of his visor was cracked. The navigation was completely unreadable. He struggled with his right arm and tapped the helmet.

Damn it. I'm completely screwed if I don't get back on course. Dom thought to himself.

It reminded him of the first time he ever jumped out of a space shuttle from Earth's stratosphere. No suit, no navigation. Just himself, a parachute, and the markers on the ground. The fall itself was great, as great as it ever could be for a seventeen-year-old who had snuck out to hitch a ride on a shuttle. The landing left much to be desired as he veered off course, slammed into a large pine tree, and hit every branch on the way down.

It was totally worth it, he thought to himself at the time, despite still finding splinters months after the stunt. His parents were rightfully angry and they banned him from even going near any sort of landing pad at the time. Julio was angry too, but only because Dom had gone without him. Dom made it up to him though, by having Julio record and distribute his attempt to jump sixteen buses with a borrowed dirt bike. The video was a massive success, mostly because Dom came up three buses short and broke nine bones all over his body.

Dom smiled. It was like the good old days before he ever had the idea of potentially jumping to his doom in the back end of the solar system. He closed in his left arm, somewhat mitigating the throbbing pain in his shoulder. He steepened his angle and fell faster towards Marina Station.

Then, just as quickly as the thunderstorm appeared, it dissipated. Below him, the clouds parted ways to a massive, brightly lit void in the clouds. Around him, big chunks of frozen, gaseous ice floated undisturbed in the sky. Dom fell into a field of diamond dust which shined more beautifully than anything he had ever seen. Tiny crystals bounced off the damaged faceplate to create a beautiful tune which resembled the sound of small, high pitched bells. The blue, so heavy and so thick before, mixed in with seafoam green to create an otherworldly, ethereal glow.

It was a beautiful sight to behold but what Dom noticed quickly was the complete and utter silence around him. The storm above had been terribly and frighteningly loud but it wasn't as unnerving as the quiet that he was falling through. No familiar rush of wind or no communications echoing through his helmet. Dom was completely alone with nothing but the sound of his own deep breaths.

For over ten minutes he fell through this massive void, keeping himself busy by brushing off more ice and attempting to repair what damage he could to his suit, with each action being as loud as a gunshot. Dom neared the end of the void when he heard what sounded like the leaking of air. His heart sank.

He looked up at the crack in his helmet. It was tiny, microscopic even, but he shuddered at thinking how much air he had lost falling for so long. Dom cursed himself and placed his gloved hand over the crack in a vain attempt to plug the leak.

"Computer, show me my oxygen levels," he said through gritted teeth.

It showed nearly fifty percent and it was dropping rapidly. Dom wasn't concerned about suffocating. Rather, at this atmospheric pressure, he was more concerned about the thick clouds turning him into human jelly. The gauges revealed he was only a few hundred meters from Marina Station.

Out of the corner of his eye, he watched as the crack split in several directions. Dom could audibly hear the high-pitched rushing of air leaking into the Neptunian atmosphere. The diamond dust, beautiful before, proved to be deadly as it widened the crack even more. Every time he breathed was a struggle as the atmospheric pressure pressed down onto his damaged suit.

Finally, the face plate split across the entire width, knocking out the entire life support system. The rest of the suit squeezed against his skin, making it difficult to move and increasing the pain in his injured shoulder. Dom deployed the flaps, slowing his descent. Out in the gaseous ether, there was no sign of the orange beacon.

Did I over shoot it? Dom thought to himself. His eyes scanned what he could through the crack and the beginning signs of tunnel vision. He couldn't have missed it; he had been keeping count of the drop since the face plate cracked. It had to be coming up soon.

Panic overtook him. Dom fell further and further into darkness. If the pressure didn't turn him into paste, the eventual heat would roast him alive like a fifty-year-old marshmallow. His thoughts turned to Julio. He wished he had said something more significant to the man who had stood beside him all these years. Regret stained his mind; something that had never crossed his mind in the years of his jumps. Was it worth killing himself? He realized he got the same rush of feelings with Julio as with any other jump. God, what I wouldn't give to be top side one more time, he thought.

Either through providence or dumb luck, the faint orange glow of the beacon flashed faintly. Dom immediately released the rip cord and engaged the parachute. His entire body jerked back, causing him to groan in pain as his shoulder was violently yanked back.

He silently drifted through thick, blue and green clouds towards the ever-brightening orange light, trying to find the landing site located on the far side of the station near the enclosed hangar. Dom blinked, trying to keep his vision straight. The pain was beginning to become unbearable.

The faded grayish visage of a massive steel wall loomed ahead. Dom put his arm up just as he crashed into the side of the wall, falling eight feet onto a solid metal grate. He laid there for a few minutes, trying to figure out whether his pelvis or his thigh bones were broken. The sound of the leaking air spurred him to slowly and painfully get up and hobble towards the nearest airlock.

To his right, he spied a gas miner waving his hand and running towards him. Dom leaned against the railing and sighed. The miner helped him through the airlock and finally inside to safety. Dom took off his damaged helmet and took a deep breath.

"Hey, buddy, what the hell are you doing outside right now?" the miner asked through his helmet.

"Dying, obviously," Dom said through gritted teeth, "Can you make contact with Nereid Satellite?"

"Whoa...is that where you came from? Are you...are you Dangerous Dominic Dominguez?" the miner asked excitedly.

"Ha. I still am, apparently." Dom looked out through the nearby airlock at the swirling Blue Inferno. It definitely lived up to its deadly reputation.

He was the first through the clouds, the highest through the clouds. Another record in his book. He leaned his head back, tired and hurt.

Dom pumped his fist in the air in victory.

A SOUL TO THE STARS

LAWRENCE DAGSTINE

Darren Spickler crouched blindly in the control chair as the soul climbed slowly. He heard John Walcott speaking with the warmth of a man who had put himself in another's place. "It's a beautiful sky," he said. "Another body, another day. Crystal clear."

"Roger that. Hitching a ride with the heart attack victim, too, huh?" Of course if the body down in the clinic had had a stroke, then the ghost might have flown the men to the moon in record time.

"Best flight fuel in the whole universe," Walcott replied simply.

At the tip of the atmosphere, when John contacted the first sphere pilot for the male soul, Darren was lost again in the strange fog of fear he had felt throughout the morning. He even glanced at the familiar instruments and the panel of warning lights, hoping for a red one that would cause the flight to abort. But there was none. He heard Ike Shepherd over the sphere's transcendental communicator. "Two-minute warning, Darren. The doc couldn't save him, so buckle up. This time's for real."

Automatically he punched the stopwatch in the titanium cockpit. As if in a dream he went through the randomized space flight routine, feeling the tense knot in his neck and shoulders draw tighter, hearing the wispy sound of his breath fighting the pressure of the oxygen in the system. Now the time was racing, and he heard Ike's voice, counting coldly at first, and then with excitement as he reached the end: "Ten seconds, boys. Nine, eight, seven..."

He flicked on the data transfer switch that would send his own sphere's telemetering information to the ground, that would enable the paranormal engineers to learn all from the flight of the dead man's soul whether he himself lived or died.

"This is a huge step for the aerospace industry," some said from the launchpad.

"We still need to take precautions when using a spirit's essence for space travel," the other, more opinionated scientists remarked. "The soul is still a fairly new kind of energy source."

"*Six seconds, five, four...*"

Darren had the moment of uncertainty that he always had just before the fixed rising point (or the *ascension*): what had he forgotten? And this time, with startling clarity, he saw his son catching up with him at the elevator to the launchpad, holding out his hands. "Daddy, why don't you just once before leaving this place, wait and ask your-self: 'Have I forgotten anything?'" The boy was smart for his years, having known his father too well.

"*Three seconds, two, one...*"

At the last moment he had a mad desire to cancel himself out of the flight and let the soul continue on its way—to heaven, hell, wherever. Cancel and claim a red light, maybe even sickness.

"*Take-off!*"

There was a final "*vrooshhh!*" and he was climbing up the molecular shaft of light at three thousand miles per minute. For a moment he sat frozen in the glaring shock of the predawn sunlight. Then he heard Shepherd's voice crackling through his communicator. "Good job, Darren. You rose fast and clear. Drifting free."

Automatically Darren reached for the sphere's booster rocket switches, and with the others in wait. Where he started in the spirit's heart, traveling to the neck and head, the others were situated in the arms or legs, working their way up to the hips and shoulders. He flicked the green switch labeled Number One, flinching as the giant downward shoves from G-Force began pummeling.

It was that hectic test flight seventeen all over again, but on this ascension, with the rocket engines from each and every sphere finally blasting full throttle for the first time, he was to undergo accelerations that would cram him back into his seat with roughly five times the force of gravity. When booster number seven lit off—which would have left the sphere on the soul's upper left side trapped inside the elbow joint—he couldn't see how sustaining the added force with booster number three and four would help. Since he had already flicked its firing stud, setting off a reaction to the other spheres, he could only sit and wait. Booster three and four burst into life with a throbbing surge that disabled part of the ascension drive and practically immobilized him. Through roaring static he heard Shepherd. "They're all lit, buddy. Give it all you got...."

He stared at the switches and dials, the panels and miniature computer banks before him, hypnotized, while his speed, along with the soul's speed, increased. Male souls were always faster for some reason than female ones, especially if the male had been strong or athletic in his lifetime. And when his sphere's speed increased, little by little, so did most of the others; Walcott, controlling the right side, was already in the forearm.

He sliced through the sound barrier in an upward angle almost instantly, part of the soul's ascension methods being the route cause, and, as the Mach and G-Force numbers slid swiftly up, he heard his sphere's air pressurizer whine like metal contorting, as if in a fierce battle with air friction at a thermal phase. The outer shell was pushing a thousand degrees, minimal, but not too far from the limit. Seen through the tiny-slitted, nine-inch thick windows above his panel, the titanium skin on the outer windowsill was glowing an orange and red melody, and closest to the cockpit. Cherry-red was the color covering the base of the sphere. He finally eased up the sphere's ascent in its present vertical course. The glow became less bright, and the numbers gradually fell. He tore his eyes back to the dials before him, and heard himself chanting his speeds to Ground Control. "All spheres' G-Force levels falling properly. Mach speed still rising. 10,000...now at 20,000... now at 40,000... reaching peak levels and ascent soon."

"That sounds about right," engineers and scientists concurred.

"Don't level off or up too fast. We only just called him a few minutes ago. The clinic hasn't even conducted an autopsy yet to be sure it *was* a coronary. We don't want to waste any of the soul's energy either. All spheres need to share of the fuel, share of the essence before you break."

When he'd heard that, he questioned them on it. "Are you sure this is ethical? Or that the soul I'm using is even powerful enough?"

"Don't worry," they assured him. "You'll be amongst the stars in no time. You're the lead astronaut this time around, and with your qualifications, that says a lot."

Shepherd and Walcott had overheard. "Hey, it's okay, buddy. Remember, there's no slingshot necessary when we do this. Once we're over the planet, we'll follow up to where your sphere is and begin disengaging, and begin letting the spirit follow its own course. Then we'll make sure every last bit of molecular fuel is dry before it *too* withers out, connect up in the cerebral cortex area, stabilize airlocks, and have ourselves a drink to celebrate."

He was still uncertain; better yet, slightly nervous. "Yeah, I…I guess I'll be seeing you guys soon enough," he said.

The grinding force of acceleration seemed to build again, as if a powerful being—no, *supernatural*—had taken over and wildly decided that he would roar even faster, forever and into the afterlife, with Darren and the others hopping along for the ride, through the trackless sky. Darren felt that if one more iota, one more ounce of thrust were added on to the cumulative push, his guts would burst through his back. Disregarding the mask by his side, he concentrated on pressure breathing and fought the oxygen cramming firmly but violently into his lungs. And still the downward shove increased.

Startlingly, he heard an engineer's voice, fading momentarily but clear: "Paranormal Consistency from Ground Control. Readings?"

Readings, my ass, he wanted to say. *I can hardly breathe; something's not right.* "I have a Mach Ascent reading of 200,000 and rising." His voice was a strained grunt. "It's now almost 250." With the soul guiding his sphere, he was traveling faster than man had ever flown. "We're over 250 now. Left the cloud masses a long time ago."

"Good," the engineer said. "Remember your simulated runs on the people who were dying in the clinic those other times and you should be just fine."

Through the mental cloudiness that was enveloping him came a warning flash. The soul was at 275,000 feet. In an instant he would be in the controllability phase, prepping to disengage the spirit and join his comrades. He had a decision to make. The arms and legs… He had to decide. Should he try it? His mind cleared. If he did, and the soul threw off his control, what of his son? His wife had died five years ago, and he really didn't have any other family but him. One little tap of pressurization and they'll most certainly know one thing: whether, as an astronaut, you're the real thing, or a phony in a flight suit.

The shimmering waves of vibration starting again, Darren's sphere was beginning to describe areas of black infinity. Just a tap, and they'd know. *He'd* know himself….

"Are you in the controllability phase?" Shepherd asked.

"Entering it now." Darren tensed his legs.

"Do you intend to check your pressurizers?"

The question lay heavily on the airwaves. The indecision was over for Darren. *You think it's that simple*, he thought. *Why not on reentry, if at all?* A strange, exultant kind of freedom suddenly possessed him. "Negative," he said clearly. "I'm taking my hands off the piloting controls." He slid his feet to the steel floor, smiling as the waves of oscillation shimmied across the sphere, secure in an almost religious faith that, if he gave the spirit's mass some head, they'd all teeter through the atmosphere at a critical altitude.

And the soul did. With a final shiver he abandoned the support of its ascension and accepted the metamorphosis into a speeding projectile in space. Moments later, after the burn-out, his own sphere became a silent ballistic missile hurtling toward that very black infinity, immutably guided in its soaring circular arc by the laws of motion. It would only be controllable temporarily, he figured, for the spheres would disengage again upon final reentry into the atmosphere, the gravity conditions leveled as if he'd never even left the launchpad.

At the moment of burn-out, he became weightless, and so did the equipment around him that wasn't bolted down. It was as if an immensely powerful behemoth had lifted an incredibly strong hand from his chest. The contrast dazed him, and far more than it had on previous flights. He heard himself automatically announce, "Burn-out. We're in free flight, guys."

The instruments swam before his eyes. Floating gently against his chair, he crossed his legs in midair and peered at the panel before him. When his vision cleared, he stared at the gravity meter. It was incredible. So carefully had his flight path been planned, and so predictable were the celestial laws of scientific force concerning the male soul, that he had almost exactly hit his point. The needle of his gravity meter was creeping downward now, as it would until he reached the top point of his journey.

"We'll be joining you soon," Walcott said. "On the minute."

"Roger," he heard Shepherd say. There would be no more reports other than one at the peak of his flight and one for the flight engineers who started out in the soul's ankles. And just before his weightless ride would end, on his *own* sphere's condition.

So now he could slip into it—the fantastic realm of space flight, the ecstatic universe of motion beyond normal motion, of complete surrender to the law that swung the stars and planets. For ten minutes he would be weightless, detached from his environment of normal gravity. For much shorter times, on previous missions, and even simulations, he had known this ultimate privilege of man, this visceral freedom, but there was somehow today a new flavor to it. He knew all at once what it was and how it felt. He had lost his fear. He had emerged from a scorched and padded grassland into clear and magnificent terrain. Floating weightless against his harness, the view of a blue and green world many miles below him, he almost shouted in relief.

The immense blackness, which he had hardly glimpsed before, had turned a thought or two about the possibilities of *this* kind of space travel. The early sun in its majesty had shone white-hot from their orbital range. He was one with the sphere in a soundless and infinite and unmoving void. Only his own breath, rasping tightly against the pressure of his oxygen, broke the reverie of silence.

He began to search the blackness for areas with the most stars. And there they were, steady and in place, in a habitat unfiltered by air. His course seemed northeasterly, and the orbit of his sphere pointed sharply at Venus, the star unwinking in the void. Seconds later he glanced at the rate of his own sphere's altitude above the Earth. With the soul's ascension complete, he would eventually slow to zero soon and decrease, and at around five hundred feet per second for each second of his flight. The same would happen when the others caught up. Still, he was proud—proud because he was the first to get there and enjoy a few moments of solace with the galactic spectacle outside his window.

The sun slashed across half his instrument panel, painting its switches and screens a glaring white. The other half, in shadow, was completely black and unreadable. And all through his sphere's cockpit this phenomenon had settled; that which was encapsulated in sunlight was in bright, harsh color, all else black. It was a black and white world, some of it incredible and of almost startling clarity.

His mind fought against its acceptance, as he floated here in a reign of absolutes, the stark onslaught of some chilling force binding; as if, naked in the limitless void, far from his environment, he was being assailed by a course of thought too cutting for the human mind to sheathe.

The other spheres soon joined him, docked, and the airlocks were given the okay. In minutes, the five steel orbs formed a docking station, where one astronaut could travel or commute between the other, and hovering just within reach of their home planet.

Walcott was the first to board his sphere, champagne bottle in hand. "Good job with the gravitational stabilization, Darren," he said, popping the cork. "Time to celebrate."

Shepherd followed him. "Hey, don't start the party without me. After all, we've only got a few hours up here until that leftover fuel from that dead guy's essence dissipates on us. We need those reserves like *any* soul for reentry, the molecular body makeup of any who have passed on from *this* life into the *next*."

Walcott laughed and started pouring, and soon the engineers joined them. "Now you know I wouldn't start a shindig without you, Ike, only things are going to be different this time upon reentry."

Darren took a seat and sipped his drink and asked, "Like how?"

"Well, this isn't a test run yet it *is*…" Walcott started off by saying, "and the scientists down at Ground Control want us to try another method. Something new they discovered about the dying soul and the living soul. Hey, I don't know much about the paranormal side to this particular flight or even the simulated liftoffs when a dude's about to kick the bucket, but I do know this: ascension and descent—what goes up one way must certainly come down the same way, or in a similar fashion. Since the living soul supposedly won't have enough proper thrust when we head back, the fuel reserves of that guy will support us like food for nurturing."

"Food for nurturing? Are you serious?" Darren was confused, but he'd learn that the experimental reentry stages he'd gone through prior to this flight would be put to good use soon enough, and when the *next* kind of soul approached from beyond the stars.

Walcott shrugged his shoulders. "I'm only a pilot." He could only explain so much.

Shepherd threw them both a conforming glance. "Ditto that." Then he picked up his champagne glass and said, "Amazing the tech we operate today. We've come a long way since Apollo or Voyager. Anyway, what should we toast to?"

Walcott stood up and said, "Let's toast to man's future in space," —and with this they raised their glasses—"and *supernatural* science."

Reentry would be a tough animal to tackle. When the spheres disengaged again and positioned themselves below Darren's, he was told by Ground Control that he had to wait for something. He'd know what it is right away, so just trust us and *wait*. But what?

From out of the blackness came a soul, smaller and shaped like a giant apple seed, in a trajectory that made it seem very much like a speeding asteroid on a collision course. It was an embryonic soul of sorts, reminiscent of the other man's essence, vibrant and full of life.

"Here comes the egg," Walcott communicated up to him. "Get ready to hitch a ride."

"The living soul is approaching in three minutes," Shepherd calculated. "Align yourself with its path and we'll stabilize ourselves to your coordinates."

"Fuel outtake on," he said, switching to standby. "I'm about to enter the fetus's heart and secure gravity upon reentry, just so the newborn doesn't turn premature and so we don't burn up the same."

Through the booster rocket controls beneath the sphere he had eased the motion arc perpendicularly, then felt the cockpit shiver as the fetus encapsulated him and the others within its molecular light. He disengaged and injected the spare fuel from the male soul, whatever was left, and saw the first thin line of atmosphere begin to work on his control's surfaces. He had regained his speed in the weightless fall, and was hurtling downward at about Mach seven when the tiniest hint of infantile resistance pulsed to his arm from the joystick. He knew that he had only moments before he truly reentered the atmosphere, and through the controllability barrier, the fetus, entering some lucky mother's womb.

He called Ground Control and said, "250,000 feet. I'm in, over."

"Damage assessment," they called back up.

"No apparent physical damage. Reentry successful."

"Roger that," Walcott's voice came back. "He carried us nice and well, Ground."

Shepherd said as if he were in the same cockpit, "You mean those rays haven't made you scared, Darren?"

Darren smiled. "Negative, Ike."

The fetus carried them to 200,000 before it went its own way. When he saw the light of the newborn streaking off, he thought about his *own* son. How life and death could be the means to man succeeding in their plight for new frontiers. Life *itself*. For an instant he fought the massive certainty of it, tense and straining, but happy nonetheless.

Soon, in the ultimate moment, he knew that he had had it all—even, finally, of being an outstanding astronaut. Impassively he watched the last, horizon-swinging mountains roll and the Space Center's runways rush toward him.

And in that last second, he had forgotten nothing because he felt his son beside him.

FINDING COSMOS 145

DIANA LEE WOODY

In the year 2169, the spaceship Cassandra carrying three astronauts, Gustav Romanoff, Chris Faraday, and Claire Spencer, prepares for lift-off. The three astronauts are seated in a circle formation facing each other excitedly waiting for their mission to start.

The mission of the crew is to find life on another planet. This is the first space mission that has occurred since the 21st century. Interest in space exploration has been non-existent since the start of the Third World War. All the money spent for scientific research had been funneled into the war effort. But with the signing of the peace treaty in 2165 came a renewed interest in space exploration. However, space exploration's not quite the same as it was before the war. Scientific research isn't funded by the government anymore. It's funded by companies. They call themselves sponsors and every company wants in on the new "search for life on other planets" trend. If there's intelligent life on another planet, every fast-food chain and fizzy drink company wants the opportunity to sell their product to that new life. That's how the Finding Cosmos 145 Project got funded in the first place and that's why Gustav Romanov is the Project Lead of the project Claire had spent the last three years working on. Although, as an Aeronautical Engineer, Gustav is qualified to run the project, he's a businessman first. Gustav Romanov is known as a man who can sell anything to anyone. So, it's only natural for the sponsors to have asked for Gustav Romanov to lead the team to find life on Cosmos 145 on the 200th year anniversary of the first Moon walk.

"Alright," says Gustav, "this is it. It's taken a long time and a lot of work on all our parts to get this off the ground. We're finally going to explore the only known Earth-like planet." Chris pipes up, "And more importantly, prove Claire's theory that intelligent life exists on other planets."

"We could learn so much from the people on other planets," adds Claire.

"And what makes you think they'll be people?" responds Gustav in his usual acerbic manner.

"They may not be people exactly like us, but it is an Earth-like planet so it's not unreasonable to assume there will be some similarities," argues Claire, "I'm sure we could find some way of communicating with them and working together for the betterment of both our species."

Gustav corrects, "Yes. That's a lovely ideal. But let's remember our sponsors. They're paying us, well actually me, to make profitable business deals with any lifeforms we happen to find."

Before Claire can respond the engines start. They all snap into position. "Prepare for take-off," orders Gustav. In a rehearsed uniform motion, the crew leans back in their chairs. Each crew member's breathing apparatus automatically moves into place. Their breathing slows until the entire crew is asleep.

As they fall into a slumber, Claire remembers a running track surrounded by a grassy hill on one side and university campus buildings on the other. Claire and Chris, on their daily jog, run side by side. Claire dashes ahead of Chris. By the time he notices her absence, she is halfway

down the track. She runs off to the grassy hill, flops on the ground, and looks up at the clouds. She can't wait to be looking for life on other planets. Chris finally catches up and flops down next to her. He catches his breath "Got a lot of pent-up energy, huh?"

"Maybe. Then again maybe you're just mad I beat you AGAIN,"

laughs Claire. "I know you. The only time you have that much energy is when you're worried about something. You're still nervous about the mission, aren't you?" asks Chris. Claire brushes him off with a shrug but Chris won't give up. He knows her too well. They grew up together, went to the same college together, joined the astronaut program together, and when the call for the mission to explore other planets came up, they naturally signed up together. He was her best friend and he knew she could obsess on things. But being her best friend also meant he could pry. In fact, he felt it was his responsibility. "What is it this time?" he inquires. "The same thing I brought up at the meeting. We're going up too early. The ship's not ready," she replies.

"You sure this isn't just a case of cold feet?" he jokes.

"No! I want to get up there as much as you do. If it were possible, I'd be ready to leave now. You know that. It's just Gustav. He's so stubborn. He's rushing the mission to please the sponsors and the simple fact is the ship isn't ready. I'm sorry I'm being so paranoid about this. But they're using 21st century technology. They didn't even have Plankian Gravitational Manifesters back then!"

"Okay," appeases Chris, "If it's important to you, we'll bring it up tomorrow at the progress meeting. Again. It's all we poor minions can do since Gustav took over as Project Lead."

The memory of the sunny day at the track fades out as she awakens to Chris tapping her shoulder. "Claire," he whispers, "You awake?"

Claire yawns, "Barely. Are we there? Is Gustav awake?"

Chris looks over to Gustav to make sure. "He's still asleep. I wanted this moment to share with you without Gustav." Claire nods in agreement. Gustav would just ruin the moment with some sarcastic remark. He may be the Project Lead, but his heart isn't in the true spirit of the mission. Gustav works for two things, money and personal glory, neither of which made any sense to Claire. She has wanted to communicate with life from other planets since the first day of her Space Studies class.

Chris points to the viewing screen. "Claire. Look. There it is. Cosmos 145. We finally made it."

"I still think it should have been named after the late great Neil Tyson DeGrasse," muses Claire.

Chris counters, "Personally I like the name. And I really like that it was suggested by some kid from our hometown. Admit it. It was good PR. It got the public interested in space exploration again, didn't it?" Claire and Chris stare out the window at the approaching planet. A big beautiful blue planet not too dissimilar from Earth. Cosmos 145, the first planet similar enough to Earth to allow for human existence, and they discovered it.

Claire exclaims, "It's so beautiful."

Chris nudges her. "Do it with me. Before he wakes up." Claire nods and smiles. It's the game they've been playing since they were kids. They recite the theme from their favorite TV show from their child-hood, Universe Explorers. They know it by heart.

Chris starts. "Heading beyond our galaxy."

Claire responds, "To search for a new-found friend."

They recite that last two lines together.

"Who, though we may be different."

"We're similar in the end."

They pause as they stare out at the approaching planet. Claire wist-fully sighs, "I hope they're friendly."

Gustav grumbles, "We have to find them first before we can start making friends with them."

Chris and Claire are startled by the sound of Gustav's voice. "How long have you been awake?" snaps Chris.

Gustav laughs, "long enough to hear you nerds do your retro TV quote."

Claire chides, "You could have told us you were awake AND listening!"

Gustav replies smugly, "Why? This was much more amusing."

"Can't you take anything seriously?" demands Claire, "Chris and I are very excited about this mission and if you can't appreciate how important this is," pausing mid-sentence to compose herself, "It's taken a long time and a lot of work by a lot of people to get this project to this point. We're finally going to prove there are other species besides ourselves in the Universe."

Gustav wants to be offended by Claire's insubordination, but deep down he admires her for being the only person he knows with the nerve to talk back to him. Regardless, he is the Project Lead and feels he needs to maintain at least an appearance of authority. "All right. Calm down," he counters, "of course I'm taking the project seriously, I'm the Project Lead, aren't I?"

"You know this was Claire's brainchild. They made you Project Lead for political reasons." yells Chris.

"So what? They wanted a scientist with a personality to charm the aliens. You think you could charm them? The best you could do is recite old TV shows to them." laughs Gustav. Claire jumps in to keep the peace. "Look guys," says Claire, "this isn't the time for battle. We're on an international project to find a new Earth. Let's wait till we land before we start recreating World War III."

Chris and Gustav grumble. They are more similar in temperament than either would like to admit. Chris breaks the silence. "Well as long as Claire's good with sharing the credit." Claire replies, "It doesn't matter who had the original idea. I'm sure I got it from old Space Vortex episodes. My only issue is I think we unnecessarily rushed the mission. But, of course, it doesn't make good PR to delay a mission."

"We would have had to wait another year if we listened to Miss Doomsday," argues Gustav.

"Alright, That's Enough, Gustav!" snaps Chris, "Leave her alone!"

"It's okay, Chris. You don't have to defend me," argues Claire, "Let's just enjoy this view and bask in the honor of being the first humans to see it." Chris and Gustav know she's right. This is not the time to argue. They are making history. They settle down and focus on the approaching planet.

Claire marvels at the sight. They're about to land on this new planet without any glitches. Maybe Gustav was right. Maybe she had been overthinking again. Suddenly, a loud banging noise is heard. The ship starts to shake. They all look to each other. "What was that?!" yells Claire.

"I don't know!" screams Chris.

The ship jolts again. They all frantically work their control stations. Nothing responds. They check all the controls again, but still nothing is working. The engines stop with a thud. An eerie quiet looms. The ship drifts just long enough to let them feel safe. After a jolt the ship descends rapidly towards the planet. The realization dawns on them. They are going to crash. "This is it! Brace yourselves," commands Gustav.

Chris grabs Claire's hand. "I'm sorry we didn't get to find your aliens."

"We're going to survive this!" yells Claire as loud as she can over the screeching of the descending ship. She doesn't know if Chris even heard her. It's too loud to hear anyone. At this point all they can do is brace themselves as their spaceship falls to the planet. Mercifully they black out before they crash.

Claire awakens in the middle of a forest. She is amazed by how similar it looks to the Shenandoah Valley where she hiked in her youth. The sun peaks through the canopy of tall pine trees. She tries to stand but she is woozy. She looks around hoping to find Gustav or Chris but sees no one. She tries to calm herself. "They could still be alive. They've just landed somewhere else. Yes. They're alive. They must be alive." She is distracted by footsteps approaching her. "Chris? Gustav? Is that you?" she calls. A young human-like girl comes from out of the bushes. Claire takes it in for a minute. Life exists on this planet and it looks human. Overcome with excitement, she gestures as she speaks, "Hello. I'm so happy to meet you. What's your name? My name is Claire." The girl looks at Claire as if she's trying to understand but says nothing. Claire reproaches herself. "You don't understand. Of course not. Why would I assume you would? But you do look like us? So, how do I make you understand?" Claire continues, "there were two others like me. We were in a spaceship." Claire draws a spaceship in the air with her arms. The girl laughs as she watches Claire until, startled by approaching footsteps, she runs away into the bushes. "Hey! Where are you going?" yells Claire, "don't be afraid. I'm sure it's just my friends."

Claire runs towards the footsteps confident she will see her friends. "Chris. Gustav. Are you okay?" She is stopped in her tracks by two human-like adults moving rapidly towards her. She resumes gesturing as she speaks, "Hello. I am from the planet Earth. Our spaceship crashed. There were two others with me. Have you seen them?"

The aliens look at each other and speak in a language Claire can't understand. They move closer to Claire and take ahold of her. "Oh, I get it now. You're taking me to my friends, right?" The female alien retrieves a needle-like apparatus from her pocket. "Wait! What are you doing?" exclaims Claire, "You don't need to do this. I'll come with you willingly." The male alien holds Claire with a firmer grip. Claire sees the needle-like apparatus coming towards her. "You don't understand. I want to be friends. I want to learn from you. We have so much to exchange." Claire squirms to get away but the male alien is too strong for her. "Hey. Cut it out. You're hurting me!" The male alien tightens his grip as the female stabs the needle into Claire's arm. "How do I make you understand? I come in peace. I'm not dangerous!" cries Claire as she loses consciousness.

Claire awakens in a comfortable room that resembles an Earth living room surprisingly up to date by Earth standards. "Could these aliens really be that similar to us?" muses Claire to herself. There are tables with Earth-like food scattered throughout the room. She tries something that looks like a grape. She cautiously sniffs it. It smells like a grape. She hesitates but she's so hungry she's willing to take the risk. She pops it in her mouth. The flavor is amazing. This must be the most delicious grape she has ever tasted. Could it be that they have the same plant life on Cosmos 145? Claire looks around at the other food table and notices a window. She grabs more grapes and heads to the window. She looks out to see what looks like a forest. "Enjoying the view?" coos Gustav as he sits up from his lounging position on the couch.

Claire turns rapidly, "Gustav! You're safe. Thank God!" She looks around the room. "Where's Chris?"

Gustav replies, "I don't know. I haven't seen him since the crash."

"What is this place? What are we doing here?!" demands Claire.

Gustav reclines back on the couch and replies. "Apparently this is our new home. And we're guests. Or captives. I'm not sure which. But either way the food is good and our quarters are comfortable."

"What do you mean captives?" demands Claire, "Who's keeping us here?" Gustav laughs. "You haven't seen them? They look like us."

"I saw a little girl alien in the forest." She looked human and I tried to talk to her but some other aliens scared her off. They looked human also. They talked but I couldn't understand them. Then one of them held me while the other sedated me. That's the last thing I remember."

"Until you woke up here," replies Gustav, "the same thing happened to me. Except I didn't see any little girl alien."

Claire moves to the door. There is no door handle. "Is this one of those automatic sliding doors?" she asks as she searches for the button to open the door.

"Don't waste your time," says Gustav, "I already tried. We're locked in."

Claire continues to search as she speaks. "Why would those people lock us in?" "You mean our hosts? First of all, they're not people," explains Gustav, "they look like us. But they aren't human." He takes a break to walk to the food table and reach for a grape. He speaks as he munches on the grape. "You know those alien life forms you were so eager to meet. Well, we found them. Or rather, they found us. And now they're keeping us here in this room." "Why? What do they want?" asks Claire.

"The best I can gather is, and keep in mind this is just a guess, we're in an observational room or zoo," replies Gustav, "at least I think so because they're always watching us." "Watching us? How?" asks Claire. Gustav walks over to join Claire at the window, picking up one of the stylish Modern Retro lamps on the way. He stands in front of the window. "Looks like a forest, doesn't it? That's what I thought until I caught the light just right." Gustav shines the lamp on the window at just the right angle. The forest disappears and theater seating appears. "Normally it's filled with them. Our hosts. Sitting out there, just watching. The only time I ever get any privacy is when I go to the bathroom. At least I hope so." He laughs. Claire, recoiling from the window, exclaims. "Watching us? Why would they want to watch us?"

"Why do we watch our animals?" he continues, "because they're interesting. And here on this planet we are the animals and apparently, we're interesting. At least that's what I'm assuming based on the data we have. If you've got a better explanation, I'm up for it." "What do they do when they watch?" asks Claire.

Gustav shrugs. "Not much. They write things down and they talk to each other. I started doing more interesting things once I noticed they were taking notes, just to see how they react. So, I guess I'm observing and studying them now."

"Maybe they're trying to determine if we're dangerous," reasons Claire.

Gustav laughs. "I think it's obvious we aren't dangerous to them. But I do think they like us. Just look at all this food. I'm sure with a little charm and smooth talking, I can convince them we can do business in the future."

"This is better than I thought," exclaims Claire, "we have found a species more intelligent than we are. We can learn so much from them. Maybe they'll want to come back with us to Earth once we repair our ship. They could even help us with that."

Gustav stops her. "You do know the ship was destroyed in the crash, don't you?" "Destroyed?" exclaims a shocked Claire, "I can't believe that."

Gustav scoffs. "Why not? You predicted it would happen."

Claire turns on Gustav, seething. "You say that like you think I wanted it to happen." "Well, didn't you? Deep down," counters Gustav, "you've been against this mission the entire time."

"How can you say that?" fumes Claire, "this entire project was my idea. I've been saying for years that a manned mission was our best hope for finding life on other planets." Gustav shrugs. "I know. That's why I can't understand why you were delaying it at every step. You should have been happy we were finally going to prove life exists on another planet." "Of course, I was happy," sighs Claire, "when they finally approved the mission, I felt all my hard work had been worth it. But the ship wasn't ready."

Gustav shrugs. "It's a moot point now. The ship crashed. Nothing is left. You were right and everyone else was wrong."

Claire collapses on the couch. She has a lot to take in. She didn't want to be right about this. Deep down she was hoping it was just her obsessive overthinking. But she WAS right. The ship wasn't ready and now it's destroyed.

Gustav walks over to the table, picks up the chocolates in a bowl on the table. He pops one in his mouth. He savors the flavor, speaking as he chews. "Chocolate raspberry. Gotta hand it to them. They know how to treat their guests."

"How can you eat bon bons at a time like this?" exclaims Claire.

Gustav picks up another chocolate and pops it in his mouth. This time he savors the chocolate with an even greater intensity just to aggravate Claire. "What else can I do? Work myself up into a lather like you. Being locked up here isn't something I'd choose. But they're feeding us, and the room is comfortable. And might I add, if they were going to kill us, they would have done so by now. Don't worry. They may be smarter than we are but I'll be running this place in no time."

Claire moves off the couch and starts to pace. She has a plan. "I need to get out of here and convince them they don't need to keep us locked up. We're here to make friends and learn from each other!"

Gustav lounges on the couch with the bowl of chocolates. "And what exactly are you going to do? Find the first aliens you see and ask them to take you to their leader? You don't know your way around or what's out there. You could get lost or hurt and at the very least insult them for not appreciating all this fine hospitality." Gustav rummages through the bowl of chocolates for his favorites. "If you want my opinion, I think we should stay here and find out what they want."

Claire is shocked. She knew Gustav was no hero but this was beyond belief. "I can't believe you're giving up that easy."

"I'm not giving up. I'm being practical. We're getting three square meals and comfortable lodging and if all they want in return is to watch me, then I'll put on a good show for them. We can always negotiate later."

"Well, I can't wait here in your little zoo. We have a mission." Claire walks around the room looking for an escape. Gustav watches as Claire checks every nook and cranny. She pushes every possible wall looking for an escape. She checks the window for its strength. She stops for a moment to reassess her options.

"Give it up Claire. We're on their clock. Enjoy being a pet. And who knows? If we're lucky, maybe they'll want us to breed," chuckles Gustav.

Claire starts to give Gustav a piece of her mind but stops. What's the point? It's Gustav. He'll never change. Gustav meanders back to the table of food and takes what looks like a chicken leg and chomps down on the meat, delighting in the flavor. In between chews he comments, "They keep feeding us like this and I'll have to go on a diet."

They both freeze when they hear footsteps approaching. It sounds like several people. The door slides open and Chris is pushed inside. Claire runs to hug him. Gustav is relieved but hides it from either one of them. "See. I told you he was okay."

After a very long hug, Claire releases Chris. She takes a breath and pummels Chris with questions. "Where were you? Did you see the ship? Did it look salvageable? Have you tried escaping?" Chris takes a moment to compose himself.

Gustav smirks "She's apparently glad to see you. I wish she had been that excited when she saw me. But no accounting for taste." He grabs the bowl of meat and walks over to Chris "Here. Have some chicken. At least I think it's chicken. Whatever it is, it tastes like chicken."

Chris, ignoring Gustav, turns to Claire, "You were right, Claire. The ship wasn't ready." "So. You think this is my fault too?" sighs Gustav.

"You made the final decision," accuses Chris.

"It was the only choice I could make," replies Gustav defensively, "you didn't know, but they were talking about scrubbing the mission. The way I see it, our mission was to prove we could find life on another planet. Well, guess what. We found life and it looks like they're treating us well. So, you should be thanking me."

Chris explodes, "Thanking you? You have no idea what you're talking about!" Chris lunges for Gustav. Gustav drops his food and readies for a fight. Claire jumps in between the two. "Stop!" cries Claire, "this is no time for fighting. We need to think of a way to get out of here. We can't stay here as pets."

"Pets?" laughs Chris, "Is that what you think we are? Pets?"

"Actually, I was thinking we're in some kind of zoo," Gustav muses, "and we're the main attraction."

Chris turns on Gustav dripping with contempt. "You're wrong again, Gustav. We're not zoo exhibits and we're not pets."

Gustav counters, "All right. Maybe not. But they obviously like us.

How else would you explain our set up here? They're feeding us well. Unless you think they're fattening us up for their dinner."

Chris tries to contain his anger for Claire's sake. "You're not too far off. And I'm not sure that wouldn't be better. But the fact is, we're lab rats. "

"Lab rats?!" exclaims Claire, "What do you mean by that?"

"That's where I just came from. They have an entire lab full of species from every corner of the Universe and we're all their lab rats," explains Chris.

Claire, ignoring the part about being lab rats, focuses on the concept of a room full of living beings from other planets. This was more than she had ever dreamed. Not just one planet with living beings but numerous living beings all gathered in the aliens' laboratory together. And she was going to get to meet them. "Life from every corner of the Universe?" she exclaims,

"Have you talked to them? What are they like? I want to see them. Talk to them. There's so much to learn."

"That's not how it works here," explains Chris, "those other beings aren't here as guests either. And our 'hosts' don't really want us to fraternize with the other species. You see, they're not collecting us for diplomatic purposes. They're harvesting different species from all over the galaxy for experiments, food, sport hunting, pets, zoos. Not any different from what we collect our so-called lesser species for."

"How do you even know all this?" asks Gustav.

"I talked to the child alien," replies Chris, "she says their planet is called Zolgan so I guess that makes them Zolgans. Her name is Orla. She's the daughter of the scientists. She visits the lab every day to help her parents do their research and feed the animals."

Claire perks up. "I saw a child alien when I awoke in the forest. I tried to talk to her but she acted like she didn't understand what I was saying."

"She probably didn't understand you," explains Chris, "none of them understood us at first. But they're a lot smarter than we are. They picked up our language in a couple hours. Now they can understand everything we say. But don't expect any conversations with them. Although they can talk to us, they don't want to. It keeps them distanced. If they communicated with us, they might get attached."

"But you said the little girl talked to you," asserts Gustav, "so, she must like you. Maybe you could convince her to keep us as pets or zoo animals."

"You're not really getting it, are you?" snarls Chris.

Gustav glibly responds. "What's to get? We're safe. They obviously find us interesting to watch. Why else would they have that stadium seating out there?"

Chris realizes this is a bit much to throw at Claire and Gustav. Neither one of them is grasping the severity of the situation. Claire is blinded by her enthusiasm and Gustav is blinded by his hubris. With great restraint Chris explains to them. "The stadium seating is so they can observe our reactions after they perform their experiments on us."

"Experiments?" scoffs Gustav, "what experiments? I've been here the whole time." "Have you been having any weird dreams?" asks Chris.

Claire shakes her head. "I haven't had a chance to sleep. I woke up in the forest shortly before they brought me here. Gustav? Have you had any weird dreams?"

Gustav hesitates, trying to recall. It's coming back to him. "Come to think of it, I have had this recurring dream. In it I'm an old man sitting at a dinner table with strangers. They all look at me like they're waiting for me to say something but no one can understand me when I do speak. The others try to speak to me but I can't understand them. But it was just a dream. It doesn't mean anything."

"Don't you understand?" says Chris desperately, "that's part of their experiment. They give us their form of dementia and try to cure us with their drugs. The dream is your brain trying to make sense out of it." Gustav sits down on the couch clearly shaken.

"How could they do something like that?" exclaims Claire, "It's inhumane. "Because they're not human," counters Chris, "we need to accept the fact that we're not on the top of the food chain here."

"If what you're saying is true then why don't I don't feel any symptoms of the experiments," demands Gustav.

Chris sighs. "You won't for now. But the other species could only take so many treatments before they died. The girl, Orla, said that's why they were so happy when we landed here. We're the sturdiest species so far."

It's finally dawning on Claire. These aliens clearly do not want to be friends. "We need to get off this planet now! Chris. Do you think you could convince the girl alien to help us escape? I'm convinced our spaceship is still out there in the forest where we crashed." Gustav snarls, "I already told you it was destroyed."

"Maybe you dreamt it was destroyed," counters Claire, "they could have been controlling your mind. It could have been part of the experiment. And even if you're right and we find the ship destroyed, maybe there's a way we can fix it. I don't know. We'll figure it out. But we have to at least try. I'd rather die trying to escape than as an experiment." She takes a breath. "So, are you guys coming with me?"

Before Gustav or Chris can answer, Orla's parents, Vohan and Zea, barge into the room. They grab Chris and Gustav. As they carry them out of the room, Claire tires to stop them but she is pushed down. The door closes and Claire is left alone in the room. Before Claire can catch her breath, the door opens and Orla enters hesitantly. Claire runs to the little girl. "Orla. That's your name, right? I know you can understand me. Please help me!"

Vohan and Zea return to the room and head for Claire. Orla scurries out of the room. Zea waves a small box over Claire's head causing Claire to lose consciousness. Claire awakens in a laboratory strapped to a chair. Orla rushes in and beelines to Claire. "I'm sorry," she whispers to Claire as she unties her.

Orla freezes when she hears footsteps approaching the lab. Orla turns to Claire. "My parents are coming to get you but I won't let them." Orla runs to the door and locks it. She turns to Claire and motions for her to be very quiet.

The footsteps stop at the door. A beep sounds but the door doesn't open. A couple more beeps and then banging on the door. Zea calls from the other side of the door. "Orla. Unlock the door." Orla stands very still watching the door.

"No! You want to hurt her!" yells Orla.

Zea, in a calm but commanding voice, explains, "Honey. We realize you've grown fond of the creatures but you can't let every one of them free. Our experiments are important." Orla pleads, "Can't I just take THIS one home?"

"Sweetheart," reasons Zea, "you already have plenty of pets. And we need this one. The creature's neurological print is very similar to ours. This could help save Grandma. You want Grandma to get better, don't you?"

"Yes. Of course," sighs Orla, "but why do we have to hurt this one to do it?" "Your father and I have told you numerous times. These creatures can't be hurt. They don't have feelings like we do."

"But you said her brain was like ours," cries Orla.

Vohan takes a deep breath to calm himself. "We realize this is our fault for letting you play with the lab creatures and get attached. But you know the policy of working in the lab. No talking to the lab creatures and no naming them. Now open the door so we can get to work." "No!" yells Orla.

"Open the door now!" demands Vohan.

Orla runs to Claire's chair and whispers, "I won't let them hurt you." Orla frantically unties Claire and looks around for a place to hide her.

Vohan has lost his patience at this point. "Orla! We've indulged you enough. Unlock the door now or you're grounded for a month and we will take away all your other pets. And what's more you will never have any more pets as long as you live in our home. Do you understand, young lady?"

Zea grabs Vohan's hand to calm him down. "Vohan. That's too harsh a punishment." Vohan snaps back, "No it's not. If she can't detach herself from these creatures, then she is not cut out to be a healer. It's a matter of priorities and if she can't get them straight now while she's young, she'll end up turning into one of those crazy Alien Activists." Orla gasps. She's never heard her father so angry before. She hangs her head, walks back to Claire, and whispers, "I'm sorry," as she reattaches her restraints.

Claire frantically begs "Orla. Please don't do this."

Orla sighs and replies "I don't have a choice."

"Yes. You do," demands Claire, "Chris said you like us. Well, I like you too. I liked you the day I met you in the forest."

Orla stops fastening Claire's restraints. "You did?"

"Yes. Of course," replies Claire, "In fact, I remember my first thought was. I like this girl. We could be friends."

Orla is hooked. She would like a friend. "Everyone thinks I'm silly for being friends with the lower species. Oh. I'm sorry. I didn't mean to be rude."

"That's okay," says Claire in a calming voice, "I understand. Just untie me. And we can be friends."

Orla smiles. "I would like that. I don't have a lot of friends. I spend all my time in the lab with my parents. I'm supposed to be a healer But I don't want to. I don't like hurting you and the other creatures."

Orla is interrupted by Vohan banging his fists on the door. He has been pushed beyond his limits. "Orla!" he shouts, "I'm going to ask you only one more time." Orla looks to the door and back at Claire. She is torn but chooses to unstrap Claire. Claire jumps up, scans the room. "Is there another exit?" she demands. Orla tries to assure her new friend that she will protect her. "You don't need to escape. I'm sure I can convince them to let me keep you as a pet." Claire shakes her head. "I can't. I'm sorry. I've got to find my friends."

"But I thought we were going to be friends," cries Orla.

Claire frantically responds. "We will be friends. I promise. As soon as I find my OTHER friends. The ones who came with me. We can all be friends. That would be nice, wouldn't it?" "It's no use Orla," shouts Vohan, "we recoded the door lock. We're coming in. That creature had better be in its chair."

Claire panics and runs looking for a hiding space. The door beeps and opens. Vohan and Zea burst into the lab. They spot Claire as she is dashing behind the lab bench. "Orla! What have you done?" screams Zea, "you've let her free. It's almost impossible to catch them" Claire darts like a frightened animal from under the lab bench. Vohan and Zea chase her around the lab but Claire manages to narrowly escape their grasp every time. "Stop it!" Orla yells, "You're scaring her."

"She's right, Vohan!" yells Zea, "you'll never catch her by yelling at her. Offer her a snack. They like snacks."

Vohan runs to the feeder and pulls out saltines. Claire is backed in the corner, scanning for an escape. Vohan speaks softly as he walks towards Claire, hand outstretched holding a saltine. "Easy now. Don't be scared. I have a snack for you."

Orla knocks over some of the lab equipment to distract her parents and nods to Claire. Claire makes a dash for the door. Just as she is almost at the door, it slams shut. Vohan grabs her. Claire struggles as he gives her an injection. Claire stops struggling. She is still conscious but can't move. They put her in the chair and strap her in. Orla grabs her father and yells. "No! Please let her go! You don't need her! You can use the other two humans!"

"We can't use the other humans, darling," explains Zea, "They didn't survive the experiments. She's the only one we have left. We have no choice. We must use her. She's our only hope to save Grandma."

Orla sobs uncontrollably. "But she's not like the other creatures! She talked to me!" Vohan checks his timepiece. He's already behind schedule and can't continue catering to a little girl's childish outbursts. "Zea. Get her out of here! She's hysterical!" Zea calmly puts her arm around Orla and proceeds to escort her out of the lab. Orla escapes and rushes to Claire. She drapes her body over Claire as if to protect her. "Please don't hurt her. She's my friend!" Zea pulls Orla off Claire and moves her toward the door. They exit and the door closes behind them. With the disturbance over, Vohan looks Claire in the eyes to make sure she's still conscious. Claire looks back with pain and anguish although she can't speak. What could she say if she could speak? Her friends are dead. She was going to be experimented on. Any dreams of peacefully interacting with the aliens were destroyed. They just saw her as a lesser species to be used for their own needs.

The door slides open. Zea walks in and stands next to Vohan. "She's settled down. I gave her a somniac. She'll sleep for a couple hours." Vohan nods. "Good. She'll come to her senses in time. This incident has made me realize that we're doing her a disservice keeping her cooped up here in the lab so much. No wonder she's not bonding with her own species. She needs real friends. Not these creatures. I think we should send her to Zolgon Youth Camp this summer. It's the

same camp I went to when I was her age. She'll get some fresh air, make some real friends, and play some camp games. You know, kid stuff. And I guarantee you she'll get her priorities straight in no time.
"

Zea sighs, "I hope so." As she sets out the instruments for surgery, Zea notices Claire struggling to speak. Their eyes lock and for a moment Zea almost believes she senses pain in Claire's eyes. She sighs a belabored breath.

"What's wrong?" asks Vohan.

"Nothing really," explains Zea, "It's just that Orla's rantings are starting to get to me. When I looked into the creature's eyes, just now, I almost felt like, I mean, what if she does have emotions and feelings like us."

Vohan snaps back. "Get that thought out of your head right now. We have work to do. We need to save your mom. Priorities. Zea. Priorities."

The surgical knife moving towards her is the last thing Claire sees as she drifts off into unconsciousness.

UNEARTHLY

KEVIN CATHY

As the starship *Genesis* finished stationing itself into jump position, a random thought entered my mind.

I can't believe it took until the year 2143 for the human race to even be first attempting mega-sonic speed in space.

I grew up watching old *Star Trek* and *Star Wars* movies from over 150 years ago. As a child, I kind of figured that we would have already conquered the ability to travel through space at unbelievable speeds. Unfortunately, I learned growing up that it had taken the world more time than necessary to get to this point. We apparently put more thought into starting wars with other countries and deciding just how much we should destroy the Earth's environment. I guess I was a little too optimistic in thinking that we were farther along than we really were.

It was these thoughts from childhood that pushed me into joining the World Aeronautics and Space Administration, or WASA, in 2130. When it was mentioned that the ability to travel billions of miles in an instant was not far off, I knew I had to be a part of it.

When I joined thirteen years ago, I had no idea that I would be one of the crew members on the first ship to perform the attempt. I thought I would have just been a guy on the ground, maybe in a monitoring role. But WASA was so impressed with my aerospace engineering capabilities that they felt I would be a helpful asset to accompany the officers assigned to the first human-led crew selected to test mega-sonic speed in space.

My mind refocused back to the present when I heard Captain Sejal Friday mention my name on the ship's intercom.

"Mr. Bradley, please confirm our coordinates in the Milky Way Galaxy's matrix to ensure we are in position to attempt the first mega-sonic jump."

I looked over at Monitor Three, reviewed our location in space, and realized we were exactly where we aimed for.

"Coordinates confirmed, Captain."

Based on years and years of testing, WASA estimated that *Genesis* could travel a lightyear (about six trillion miles) in twenty hours while in mega-sonic mode. Technically, at that speed, we could reach the Andromeda Galaxy in approximately 6,250 Earth years. Of course, we'd be dead and our ship would run out of fuel by then. But if we were able to fine-tune the process even more via future experiments, we would maybe be able to cut that time into something that's actually achievable within a human's lifetime. The possibilities are endless. The universe is slowly yet quickly becoming within our reach. And I'm more than excited to play such a huge role in this initial undertaking.

I heard Lieutenant Marie Ocampo over the intercom say that engines were a go.

My engineering room began to light up all over the place. Monitors were changing screens. The jump to mega-sonic speed was fast approaching.

Captain Friday announced, "All crew staff, assume jump positions in your work areas."

I strapped myself in.

All staff checked in to confirm their positions.

Monitoring Officer, Lieutenant Marie Ocampo: "Assumed."

Pilot, Ensign Dean Caffey: "Assumed."

WASA Communications Liaison, Lieutenant Michelle Arrowhead: "Assumed."

Onboard Engineer, Civilian, Mr. Sebastian Bradley (aka: Yours Truly): "Assumed."

Second in Command, Commander Charles Boozer: "Assumed."

Captain Sejal Friday: "Assumed," followed by "Initiating jump sequence in 3… 2… 1…"

Before the indescribable jolt was felt by all, I said aloud to no one in particular, "Here goes nothing."

My head ached. It was worse than any migraine I've ever had.

I saw only the color white.

I attempted to close my eyes before realizing that they were already closed.

There was no relief from the vast whiteness surrounding my eyesight.

As the intense pain in my head began to slowly subside, images of tall buildings began to appear. Above these buildings was a sky that blended the white light with the color blue.

I was looking up from the ground of a city street's point of view.

I realized my body was lying down.

I blinked about ten times before moving my head from side to side. The migraine was now completely gone; overwhelming confusion had taken its place.

"Where the hell am I?" I managed to say aloud.

No answer was provided.

A cool breeze sifted vertically across my body. The ground began to feel cold on my back.

I found the strength to stand up and look around. I was standing amongst tall buildings in every direction.

There was no movement in sight. No ground cars on the street or flying cars above me. The area was completely void of any life.

I was alone here, wherever "here" was.

I jumped almost a foot in the air when my name was shouted as if out of nowhere.

"Bradley! Bradley! Come in, Sebastian! Can you hear me!?"

It was my communicator implant.

I touched my right temple to answer the voice.

"Bradley here. Captain Friday, is that you?"

"Affirmative," she replied. "State your location."

I looked around.

"Uh… I have no idea, Captain. There's a bunch of buildings in every direction. I'm on a city street."

Silence ensued.

After a few moments, I began to worry that my communicator was broken. Before carrying out the daunting task of removing and fixing the implant, Captain Friday finally responded.

"Bradley, are there street signs nearby?"

I searched. In the distance, I saw the names of a cross street up ahead.

"Yes, I see them. It looks like I'm on the corner of 44th and Main."

Immediately, I heard Lieutenant Ocampo speak up. "Bradley, we're on 42nd and Main. Turn the corner and head down Main Street. We're heading your way and we'll meet you at 43rd Street, over."

"Copy that," I replied.

I raced down to the corner and made the turn. I could see all of my crewmates in the distance heading toward me. They looked the same as when I last saw them; however, their facial expressions did not exhibit the same positive anxiety they possessed only moments ago aboard the *Genesis*.

When we reached each other, I asked them, "Where the hell are we?"

"I have no idea," Ensign Caffey said.

We looked around, to the ground, to the sides, and up above. Nothing but buildings in sight underneath the blue sky.

"It looks like we're back on Earth. It looks like Manhattan," Ocampo decided.

We all nodded our heads in agreement before shaking them in disbelief.

Commander Boozer stated what everyone was thinking, "This makes no sense."

The captain seemed to be inside herself; thinking before speaking was an attribute I was accustomed to her having. We all looked to her for guidance despite the fact that she did not appear ready for questions or orders.

She looked back at all of us.

"I don't know what to make of our situation," she said. "Regardless, we need to utilize our military background to institute the basic procedures for survival in a foreign land. Before we can even begin to figure out where we are or what to do, we need to satisfy the basic three human needs: water, food, and shelter.

"Ocampo, Caffey: Scope the general area for possible water sources.

"Arrowhead, Boozer: Look for food.

"Mr. Bradley, you're with me. Let's see if we can break into one of these buildings.

"Everybody, set your communicator implants to group function so we can be linked in with each other at all times.

"Are your orders understood?"

We all responded with "Yes, ma'am!"

She nodded before yelling, "Move out!"

While working with the *Genesis* crew over the last few years, I had never really witnessed them executing their military bearing. There was never a need. However, apparently it was something ingrained within each of them because they were all now acting and speaking like officers in combat. Being a civilian, I was unsure of how to act within this now somewhat formal military unit. As such, I decided to just be and talk like my normal self.

The crew had dispersed in their own directions while I walked with Captain Friday.

We both looked around before she asked, "Which one of these buildings do you think would provide sufficient shelter?"

As I scoped out the different buildings, I noticed one that resembled more of an apartment complex than anything else.

I pointed to it and said, "That one looks promising."

Captain Friday's worrisome yet determined eyes met with the building I pointed out. She examined the look of it before saying, "Nice choice. Let's check it out."

We headed towards the building, feeling gusts of cold air moving through us.

When we arrived at the possible apartment building's entrance, Captain Friday reached out to open the door.

It was unlocked.

Before the door could be pushed open, a blaring scream was heard inside my implant.

"Report!" Captain Friday demanded.

"We're under attack!"

At first, I couldn't make out whose voice it was because the shouted words were so erratic. It was only until I heard the voice continue with "Commander Boozer is dead" that I realized it was Lieutenant Michelle Arrowhead's voice.

Friday's eyes widened with fear, as did my own.

"Attention all crew members: Report back to 43rd Street to regroup!"

"Affirmative!" they all replied in unison.

What felt like only a second later, we were all back on 43rd Street, minus one.

"What the hell happened, Arrowhead?" Friday questioned.

Michelle was noticeably shook up and appearing to do her best to maintain her composure.

"It came out of nowhere! I... I don't know what it was... what it is. It was dark – not human. It was tall, like... fifteen feet. It... It didn't even touch him. It just opened its mouth... if that's what it was... and just... sucked the life out of him. Boozer screamed and then just collapsed. I couldn't revive him. It was like the figure ingested his *soul*... I just can't explain it."

Her attempt at sounding professional and tough completely disappeared as she started to cry. The rest of us looked at each other with immense concern.

Before we could process what all had just occurred in the last ten minutes, a familiar voice came through our implants.

"*Genesis*, please come in... *Genesis* crew, *Genesis* crew; this is WASA Headquarters; please come in."

Captain Friday immediately touched her temple. "This is Captain Friday. WASA, can you hear me?"

"Loud and clear, Captain. Report your status, over."

Friday took a second before replying, "WASA, I honestly don't know how to explain our situation. We are no longer in space... We appear to be in New York City on 43rd and Main Street, but there are no people in sight. Commander Boozer was attacked and killed by an alien being. We have no idea what's going on..., over."

Radio silence ensued for what felt like hours.

"Standby, *Genesis*."

Another long moment of silence continued.

None of us spoke to each other. We looked all around dispassionately, hoping not to see the vile creature that Arrowhead had described.

"*Genesis* crew, come in."

"We're here," Friday responded.

"*Genesis*, we have spoken with various experts here at Headquarters. There is a physicist here who thinks he knows what has happened. I'll let him explain."

"*Genesis* crew, can you hear me?" came a voice we've never heard before.

"Yes," Captain Friday replied.

"Captain Friday, my name is Dr. Gerald Mead. I know you and your crew have some physics education, but probably not at my level. I could give you my assumption in extremely complex terms that would take hours of explaining, but I won't; I'll just give it to you straight.

"Essentially, when your ship attempted to jump through space using antimatter materials at an untested magnitude, an explosion occurred at the multidimensional level. It seems that the explosion tore a hole in subspace allowing for all life near it to be enveloped and able to pass through to a parallel universe.

"You are back on Earth, but on an Earth that is different than the one you are from. Those alien creatures you mentioned are likely the dominant species of Earth in that particular universe. If you think about it from their point of view, *you* are the aliens."

It took quite a bit of time to digest this man's theory. At first, I completely dismissed the notions. But the more I thought about it, the more it made sense.

"So," Captain Friday spoke, "how do we get out of here?"

"I have an idea," Dr. Mead responded. "But it's pretty wild."

"Wilder than entering a parallel universe with soul sucking aliens trying to kill us on an otherwise empty Earth?" Ensign Caffey said with disdain.

"Okay, I guess my solution is on the same level," Dr. Mead replied. "Here's my theory: The fact that you and your crew ended up on an alternative Earth and the fact that we're still able to communicate with you, I believe you're not too far away from your original location on the multiverse spectrum. Creations that are made here on the Earth that you are from appear to be present in your current location as well. In other words, there should be a working *Genesis* starship at the same location as the one you left from. You said you are in New York City on 43rd and Main Street, correct?"

"Yes, sir."

"Then you're about ten miles from the WASA station. I recommend you get your asses back to the *Genesis* ship in your universe, launch into space, and reconvene back at the same coordinates that you just left before the attempted first jump. At that point, perform the same exact jump sequence to mega-sonic speed to pass back through the same subspace hole you first entered. There's a chance you may pass into another different universe, but I'm pretty sure you should arrive back at the same universe you originated from."

It took a minute to process all that we heard before Captain Friday responded with "Heard and understood. Proceeding to the *Genesis* launch site, over."

Without speaking, we began walking down Main Street towards the direction of the WASA Station.

It had been a while since I had been in downtown New York, but all of the buildings looked familiar. Besides the lack of any other human life, this place didn't seem or feel different at all.

After about seven miles of walking in total silence, we began crossing the bridge.

While reaching the halfway mark on the bridge, a loud splash was seen and heard to the right and underneath us.

A creature began to slowly emerge from the water.

It looked exactly like what Michelle Arrowhead tried to describe.

It was dark and monstrous.

It floated above the water and let out a blasting scream.

I don't know who yelled "Run!"

It may have been me.

As we ran across the bridge, I looked behind and saw the creature flying towards us and closing in fast.

Lieutenant Ocampo was slightly in front of me until she tripped. I had to jump over her to make sure I didn't fall over too.

I stopped to turn around and bent down to help her, but the creature came upon us so quickly that I backed away just as fast.

Ocampo's terror stricken eyes burned into my permanent memory. I knew at that moment, as I witnessed her life (and possibly her very soul) being drained, that this occurrence and all the emotions that came with it would haunt me for the rest of my days.

After Ocampo was completely still, the creature, apparently satiated, flew upwards and then back into the water from whence it came.

"Keep running!" Captain Friday yelled.

We ran for at least two miles before stopping in an alleyway to catch our breaths.

We heaved for a few seconds before Arrowhead said, "We're almost there."

Captain Friday looked ahead and pointed. "There it is."

We looked in her direction. In the distance, we could see Mission Control.

More importantly, we could see our ship docked and ready to be launched.

I finally gained the courage to chime in with my militaristic group.

"Let's go."

~

We arrived at the WASA station without further incident. Like the city of New York, this station looked exactly the same as the one I remembered in our original universe. This world was basically identical to our own, minus the lack of people and the occupancy of soul sucking demon-like creatures.

We boarded the ship and began turning on all of the instruments.

"WASA, can you still hear us?" Friday asked through our communicator.

"Still here, *Genesis*. What is your status?"

"We're aboard the ship. All systems are almost up and running."

"Understood. Prepare for launch sequence."

"Report to your stations," Captain Friday instructed.

I rushed to my engineering room.

It was the same room I was in only hours ago.

I was repeating the same process I had done earlier today.

My monitors were all turned on and ready for ignition.

"Initiate launch engines," I heard over the ship's intercom.

~

In what felt like no time at all, we were back in space; back at the same place we had been only hours ago.

"Mr. Bradley," Captain Friday said. "Please confirm our coordinates in the Milky Way Galaxy's matrix to ensure we are in position to attempt the mega-sonic jump."

I looked over at Monitor Three, reviewed our location in space, and realized we were exactly where we aimed for.

"Coordinates confirmed, Captain."

"Engines are a go," I overheard Ensign Caffey state on the intercom.

My engineering room began to light up all over the place. Monitors were changing screens. The jump to mega-sonic speed was fast approaching... again.

Captain Friday announced, "All crew staff, assume jump positions in your work areas."

It was disheartening to not hear Lieutenant Ocampo's or Commander Boozer's voices after the surviving crew and I responded with "Assumed."

"Initiating jump sequence in 3... 2... 1..."

Before the familiar jolt, I said aloud to no one in particular (for the second time today and in a different universe), "Here goes nothing."

～

My head ached, worse than it did before.

It felt as though my brain was continuously imploding.

Again, I could only see the color white until basic colors slowly started to formulate. The immense pain began to diminish as my eyesight became more pronounced.

I was still in the engineering room.

Did we make it back to our own universe?

I looked out the window and saw the buildings of New York City as well as people, *human beings*, assembling outside.

～

As soon as we opened the ship doors, I felt elated to see a world of people again.

People were applauding on the street and on the bridge as we exited the WASA Station.

There was a gathering of people being held in the street to obviously celebrate our safe return (except of course for Ocampo and Boozer).

I was filled with too many emotions.

Unfortunately, only one of those emotions surfaced and remained when I looked at what was happening in the water below.

The dark figure, the same menace we encountered in the last parallel universe, appeared.

I screamed.

The man next to me gave me a confused look.

"Why are you screaming?" he asked.

I couldn't believe his question.

I pointed to the demonic figure which was now floating in the sky above everyone.

The man, still confused, said "Come on, man. You need to bow down. Get on your knees."

It was then that I realized that everyone was on their knees with their heads down to the ground.

The celebration had stopped. Utter silence ensued.

Not knowing what else to do, I dropped to my knees and looked to my colleagues next to me. They looked as confused and scared as me.

"God bless the guardians!" everyone said in unison.

The man next to me whispered, "Oh man, I hope he picks me this time."

I was beyond baffled.

The only notion I could imagine that happened was that my crew and I returned back to a similar yet definitely different parallel universe. Unlike the last universe, human beings actually existed on this Earth. However, just like the last universe, the demonic creatures were the dominant species. It seemed as though people on this Earth were their followers, slaves, food...?

The creature floated closely over me and I squeezed my eyelids shut, waiting for my soul to be sucked completely out.

I heard and then saw the man next to me being lifted up into the air.

He seemed happy.

"I've been chosen! God bless the guardians!"

The creature then opened its horrid mouth and ingested all the life out of the man.

The man's body was then thrown into the Atlantic Ocean.

Everyone except me and my crew stood up and began to clap.

RETURN OF THE FELINEDAENS

DEBBIE DE LOUISE

Author's Note: This is a sequel to "The Felinedae Mission" that appeared in the Red Penguin Collection's What Lies Beyond and Stand Out, Vol. 1.

New York City, 2031: They're baaaack!

Jezebel woke me up by jumping next to my pillow and meowing in my ear. Reverting to our telepathic communication, she said, "Lily, wake up. They're coming back."

I was drowsy. It was Sunday. The previous night I'd been out with my friends from the cat club celebrating my fortieth birthday. It had been Amanda's idea to throw a surprise party for me at her apartment. The four of us were up until the wee hours reminiscing, eating, and drinking. She'd even baked me a cat-shaped birthday cake with pawprints on it. Valerie brought balloons with "40" on them and a crown to put on my head. Norman supplied the liquor.

"Leave me alone, Jezzy," I said, turning to face away from her calico face and those accusing green eyes.

"Don't you even want to welcome them home?"

"Welcome who home?" Then I realized who she was talking about. In February of 2030, my two male cats, Jake and Joey, were taken by an alien from the planet Felinedae. While their leader,

Catling, and her followers had abducted other cats in the same way, they had wiped the memories of that night from humans all over the world. It was still hazy to me, although some of it came back in dreams, and some of it was filled in by Jezebel. My most recurring dream was of taking the subway with Amanda, Valerie, Norman, and our cats and going to my sister Laura's house where we watched President Young's broadcast of the alien invasion. Laura had been pregnant at the time and now had a two-year-old son, Todd, jr., who'd joined his older sister, Kerri, who was now ten years old.

I turned back to Jezebel. She was grooming herself, licking her white paws and stomach. "Are you talking about your brothers? Why are they coming back?"

She paused in her cleaning and looked at me again through her big green eyes. "Sorry. I made a mistake. Joey is the only one coming back. Catling is keeping Jake."

Joey, Jezebel's black littermate, would now be her same age — six years old. Jake, my mackerel tabby, had been the older cat. He would be eleven. "Why is Catling keeping Jake?"

Jezebel didn't reply. It was frustrating when she went silent on me.

I persisted in my questions. "When is Joey coming home? Are other cats being reunited with their owners, too? Talk to me, Jezzy."

She just rolled over and showed me her tummy. I resisted the urge to pet it. "Fine. Have it your way, but no treats for you today."

That elicited a response. "I've been in touch with Joey. He said that a few cats are returning with him. They're bringing the antidote."

"Antidote for what?" This was getting too mysterious.

"The plague. Coronavirus 3. This one would kill everyone."

I gasped. I recalled how COVID-19 had spread worldwide from 2020 to 2023, mutating in dozens of variants and killing millions of people until it suddenly disappeared. My fiancée was one of those who had succumbed to it. I was thirty then and engaged to Robert who had diabetes. I spent weeks in the hospital watching him drift away on his ventilator. I'd caught a less severe case toward the end of the pandemic when vaccines had become available, but I'd still suffered fever, chills, with congestion and a cough that lasted for months. Scientists couldn't explain how it finally died out, but everyone was relieved. People felt safe gathering in crowds again. They threw away their face masks.

"What are you talking about, Jezzy?"

"It's coming, Lily. This time, Catling can't disperse the antidote over the Earth as she did last time. It has to be delivered by the cats. Joey has trained a year and a half for this."

I didn't understand. There had been no reports of a new virus in eight years, but I knew that things were often covered up in the beginning or not identified immediately. But just as I was about to ask more questions, I heard a meow by the bedroom door. I turned to see Joey's dark form standing there, his golden eyes alight with a strange glow.

"Hello, Lily. I see Jezebel has been filling you in on my mission."

I was shocked. I'd only been able to communicate with Jezebel in the past, but now I could clearly hear Joey's voice, a deep baritone, in my head.

I got off the bed as I watched the two cats touch noses. "Welcome home, Brother," Jezebel said.

I was scared of approaching Joey. He looked the same except for his eyes and the fact that he was now a telepath.

"Don't you want to pet me?" he asked. "Have you missed me?"

I approached him slowly. As Jezebel stepped back, Joey wrapped himself around my bare ankles, purring.

I reached down and picked him up. I cuddled him close to my nightshirt. "Oh, Joey. Yes, I've missed you. Tell me what happened? Tell me about your mission. How is Jake?"

In between purrs, he said, "I haven't seen Jake. He was placed in a different division. I can't reveal all the details of my mission. Catling has forbidden that. However, I want to give you protection against the virus." He drew a breath and, as he exhaled, he blew it out on my face. I coughed as I inhaled the fishy smell. "Joey, what have they been feeding you?"

He laughed. "We get the best food up there. I had salmon for breakfast."

"I can tell, but am I now immune?"

"You are, and just in time. The virus is about to hit."

"When will that be?"

"Shortly. It's on its way. Please put me down and turn on your TV or computer. You'll see what I mean."

I let Joey down and did as he asked. I booted up my laptop which I kept on my bureau. I used it for writing my mystery series and sometimes also for my work as a librarian at the New York Public Library.

When I logged into a news site, I saw a red headline flash across the screen. "Breaking News: Signs of a New Virus Warn of an Upcoming Pandemic." I clicked on the link that led to a streaming video. Jonathan Wolf, current head of the CDC, was speaking. I toggled up the sound.

"At this point, there's no need to panic, but we have identified a few cases in California and the West Coast as a new strain of virus, similar to COVID-19, but more contagious and more likely to cause severe reaction. We are following the progression of this disease carefully. For now, we recommend avoiding crowded gatherings unless you wear a face mask or shield. Further updates will follow."

A burst of questions was shouted by reporters and dozens of comments scrolled by in the chat. I turned back to Joey. "So, what's the plan? Jezzy says that other cats are coming down from Felinedae to help eradicate the virus."

"Yes. The cats who were taken a year and eighteen months ago will be returning to their owners and immunizing them as I just did you."

"But what about the other people—the ones whose cats weren't taken or ones who don't have cats?" I was thinking of my friends, sister, and mother.

"The Immunizers, as we call ourselves, will share our breath with other cats, too. We have also been assigned non-cat owners, but there may be difficulties involved in helping them because some are allergic and won't allow us into their homes."

I still wasn't comprehending. "What's so special about your breath? It smelled like regular cat breath to me—salmon and all."

"While we were on Felinedae, we were feasting on special substances that built up our immune systems and are transferred by breath to humans."

Jezebel spoke then. "Tell her about the COVID-19, how Felinedae knocked it out."

"I was getting to that, Sis. Eleven years ago, when COVID first hit,

Catling had communication from some cats who were researching Earth. She set out to find a cure, something none of the scientists and doctors could do despite vaccines and boosters. When she perfected this cure, she was able to send it to Earth via a few spaceships. It was an invisible powder that blanketed the planet and got into its waterways and air."

"That sounds amazing," I said, "but why didn't Catling tell us this when she abducted you and the other felines instead of putting the humans to sleep? Had we known of the great service she'd done for us, we would've welcomed her and her companions."

Joey walked toward the cat tree in the bedroom's corner and jumped on top of it. He faced me and replied, "I don't know why she chose to do it that way, but perhaps she felt no one would believe her."

"So, what about now?" I persisted. "How come she can't just spread the antidote over the Earth again? Why do you cats have to be involved?"

Joey licked his right paw and began cleaning himself. "I don't have all the answers, Lily, but this new virus didn't respond to the ingredients Catling used previously. She heard about the virus a few years ago and has been working on the cure. Luckily, she found it before it became a pandemic."

Things were making sense now. "So, that's the real reason she abducted you cats a year and a half ago."

Joey was cleaning his chest. Jezebel began mimicking him, as she used to do when they were kittens. She also joined him on the cat tree, taking the second level.

"You got it. When she figured out she needed us to spread the cure, she had to take us to begin our diet regimen."

I had one last question. Walking over to the cat tree, I asked, "How did Catling learn about the virus before it started?"

"Can't you figure that out? Catling is a superior being from another world. She can see the future of our world, as well as yours."

After a pause, Jezebel said, "If you're done with the twenty questions, can we eat now?"

I laughed. "Come into the kitchen, and I'll put out your food. Are you able to eat cat food now, Joey?"

He jumped off the tree. "Yes. Regular feline food won't interfere with my immune breath."

"Oh, brother," Jezebel said, rolling her green eyes as she leaped down from the tree, and both cats followed me into the kitchen.

As the cats chowed down, I thought of more questions, but I was afraid to voice them because Jezebel might admonish me. I laughed at myself for being afraid of a cat. There were things I needed to know about this virus-killing antidote.

"Sorry to disturb you, Joey, but how long does this feline breath protection last and how many people can you deliver it to? Is there a limit?"

Joey looked up from his food bowl, a smear of cat food on his dark furry lips. "The protection is lifelong, but I can only administer twelve doses."

I did a count of my family and friends in my head, including their cats—my mother, sister Laura; my brother-in-law, Todd; their daughter Kerri; baby son, Todd, Jr., and cat Garfield; my friends; Amanda and her cat, Charlie; Valerie and her Scottish Folds, Biscuit and Cookie. That came to eleven, and I had already had a dose.

"Perfect," I said. "You can take care of everyone who is close to me."

"Aren't you forgetting somebody?" Jezebel asked, batting Joey away from the food, so she could sneak a nibble.

"Cats are naturally immune to the virus, unlike the COVID some caught back in 2020, although most didn't have major reactions. The only reason I give the cat breath to other cats is for them to spread it to others."

"Does that mean, once you deliver all the feline breaths, you no longer possess the antidote and have to return to Felinedae?" I was hoping Joey could keep living with me, and maybe Jake would come home one day, too.

Joey stopped chewing. "No. That's not it, Lily. If I use up all the cat breaths, I die."

I gasped. "How awful!"

Jezebel said, "Let me get this straight, brother. You have twelve cat breaths. After that, you can't give away anymore or you'll croak."

"I'm afraid so."

"Then we'll be very careful. According to my calculations, although I've never been great at math, you can immunize my relatives and friends and also their cats without using your thirteenth breath."

Jezebel had another question. This one was for me. "Lily, how is Joey going to immunize your mother? Doesn't she live in California?"

I'd already thought about that. "She's coming here, Jezzy. I invited her to visit this week. She should arrive tomorrow."

Jezebel gave me an angry stare. "Why am I just hearing about this? The last time Mrs. Palmer was here, she said you were feeding me too much, and her breath stank."

"Look who's talking," I pointed out, but I knew she was referring to my mother's alcoholism, a vice she'd picked up after my father perished in the 9/11 terrorism attack on the World's Trade Center. "You could afford to lose a few pounds, Jezzy, and my mom has been on an AA program. She's doing well."

"Good to know," Joey said. "But what are our plans for today?. Time is of the essence."

It so happened that we had a cat club meeting scheduled that afternoon. My three friends and I met monthly to talk about our cats. "Amanda, Valerie, and Norman are coming over later. You can give them your breath then. They'll be happy to see you back. They also bring their cats."

"That works." Joey walked away from his food dish. "What about your sister and her family and cat?"

"They'll come tomorrow to see my mother when she arrives after I pick her up from the airport."

It was then that I realized I hadn't shut off the television, and the news was still broadcasting. An announcer said, "Breaking News. We've just been informed that the first case of COVID 3 has been diagnosed in a New York City resident. More details will be disclosed as soon as we have them. Stay tuned to News On the World."

"You're right. You're back just in time," I told Joey.

He let out a big purr of agreement.

. . .

The cat club members began to arrive for our lunchtime meeting at twelve noon. Valerie arrived first with Biscuit and Cookie in their carriers. She was dressed in her usual bohemian styled long patchwork skirt of earth-toned colors. Gold chandelier earrings dangled from her lobes. Her lips held just a touch of beige gloss. "Hey, Lil, is that Joey I see? I thought he disappeared over a year ago."

"He's back. I'll fill you in when everyone gets here."

She gave me a quizzical look and shrugged. "I'm sorry, but I forgot to bring something." Each member of the club brought food or drink to the meetings.

"That's okay. I have a refrigerator full of food. My mother is coming over tomorrow to stay awhile."

"That should be fun." She was being sarcastic.

Biscuit and Cookie cried simultaneously, so she released them from their carriers. Jezebel and Joey approached them slowly. Joey went up to Biscuit's face and breathed into it. The cat jumped back. I was afraid they would fight, but Joey moved quickly over to Cookie and repeated the action.

"What are they doing?" Valerie asked.

I couldn't resist teasing her. "You're the behaviorist. You tell me."

She smiled. "Funny, Lily. It's a good thing my Scotties are so well behaved and haven't scratched Joey's face."

"Your Scotties will thank him later."

"You're being mystical again. Wait. I hear Amanda. At least I hear her heels."

Amanda loved shoes, especially high ones, because she, like me, was vertically challenged.

Sure enough, a knock followed the sound of boots at my door. I went to answer it. Amanda stood there holding Charlie in his cat carrier in one hand and a covered Tupperware cake carrier in the other. "Am I late?" she asked.

"No. Norman's not here yet, and Val came early." I took the cake from her. Through the opaque top, I could see it had chocolate icing. "Looks yummy. Thanks."

She smiled. Dressed all in black except for white knee-high boots and a white scarf around her neck, my vet and friend matched her tuxedo cat, Charlie.

She stepped into the kitchen as I put away the cake and waved to Valerie. As soon as she opened the cat carrier, Joey breathed into Charlie's face. He wasn't as mannerly as the Scottish Folds and hissed at my cat.

"What in the world?" Amanda said. "I thought Joey was gone."

"We all did, but he's back."

"But why did he blow on Charlie?"

"She's not telling us yet," Valerie said. "She did the same thing to my boys."

"I have to wait for Norman."

"And here I am," came a voice from behind my front door. Norman let himself in. "Hi, Ladies." Since he still hadn't replaced his dead cat, he held no cat carrier. Instead, there were two bottles of wine in his arms, one red; one white.

"Welcome," I said, "thanks for bringing the drinks. We're gonna need them."

"Uh, oh. What does that mean, and is that Joey over there?"

"Yes, it is. Have a seat, and I'll explain everything."

"It's about time," Amanda said, drumming her long black nails on the table.

"I'll save Lily the trouble," Joey said. I knew he was speaking telepathically to me, but the others turned to look at him.

"Did that cat talk?" Valerie asked.

"I heard him," Amanda replied.

"We haven't even had a drink yet," Norman added.

If I could've captured my friends' shocked expressions as they listened to my cat's story, I could've gone viral on any social media I posted it to. What really blew their minds was when their own cats spoke up. It surprised me, too, because Joey had neglected to explain that perk of his cat breath.

When the cats stopped speaking, there was a long silence until

Norman broke it. "I think I'll open these bottles now. Got an opener, Lil?"

As I went to a drawer to get it, Amanda said, "You've really outdone yourself, Lily. I almost fell for it. When did you take up ventriloquism? That must be how you're doing their voices. I like the Scottish folds with their delightful accents, and Jezebel sounds as prissy as I imagined she would. Great job."

Valerie said, "That must be it, Amanda. I almost believed it, too. Cats from a planet called Felinedae? Lily, you have quite the imagination."

I never thought I'd have trouble convincing them, but I should've known that they had no recollection of what happened eighteen months ago when Catling took Joey. Norman seemed the only one who might consider the possibility that I wasn't jesting with them. As he opened the wine bottles and poured glasses all around, he said, "I don't think Lily is projecting her voice into the cats or tricking us in another way. It's too crazy not to be true."

"It is true," Joey said, "believe me, if Lily was making me talk, I wouldn't sound this way."

"Okay, if this is true," Amanda, ever the behaviorist, said, "do we just let you breathe on us?"

"That's the plan," Charlie said, approaching his lady. "Along with the breath, Joey has transferred to us cats all the training that Catling gave him and his telepathic abilities. It doesn't work that way with humans. It merely imparts immunity to the virus." He jumped on her lap and blew in her face. "There you go. You'll survive now."

"Ugh!" Amanda explained. "I shouldn't have given you that tuna today. Seriously, am I now immune to the new pandemic?"

"Yes, my dear lady. Pet me to show your appreciation."

"This is too much," Valerie said, as Cookie and Biscuit both blew into her face.

"Don't do that," Joey yelled. "You'll waste your breaths."

"They have twelve," I pointed out.

"Not exactly."

"What do you mean?" Was there something else Joey had neglected to tell me?

"The cats who give the breath, the ones Catling trained and fed for eighteen months with the immunity-providing nutrients, have twelve breaths, but the normal cats who receive it only have one."

Biscuit and Cookie gave him an astonished look, their folded ears almost flipping up. "That means that's it for us? If we give another breath, we die?"

"That's the way it sounds, fellas," Jezebel said. "I don't even want that stinking breath."

Norman said, "One of you could've given it to me. I don't even have a cat anymore."

"Don't worry," Joey said. "I have eight more breaths. Here's one for you, Norm." At that, he jumped up on the scientist's lap and blew into his face.

"Thank you, but I really can't see how that will protect me. It's not a vaccine."

"No, but it will grow in your lungs and stop the virus from entering your body."

Norman shrugged. "If I believe all you cats can talk, I have to believe your breath has immunized me."

Joey stuck his chest out proudly as he strutted to my side. "Now we just have to convince your mother and sister."

My mother's flight to JFK was on time, and I waved to her as she came off. She looked younger. I was proud of her for her one-hundred days sober.

She gave me a hug. "Lily, it's so good to see you. Did you know there were some people on that plane wearing masks? What's going on?"

I thought she may have already heard about the new pandemic, but I hated to be the one to break the news if she hadn't. Still, she'd hear of it soon enough from my cats. I changed the subject. "Do you have to go to baggage claim?" She was only carrying her purse and a small tote. I took the tote from her.

"What do you think? I'm staying for a week."

I recalled how my mother tended to overpack, but I didn't mind. It was good to have her visit."

After we'd picked up her two cases, and we rolled them to my car in the airline parking lot, we drove to my apartment. There was a lot of traffic getting out of the airport, so as we were stuck in it, I decided to start filling her in.

"Mom, there's something you should know about my cats."

"Your cats? I thought you only had Jezebel. The other two ran away. Male cats do that sometimes."

"Joey and Jake were neutered, and they didn't run away. They were taken."

"Someone stole them? I'm sorry, Lily. I know they go after cats for lab experiments."

"That's not what happened, Mom, although they were part of an experiment." I didn't know how to tell her the rest, but I'd come that far.

"What then? They weren't pure breeds."

"Well, it's a long story and a strange one. But the main thing is that Joey is back, and you know how you saw the passengers with masks? Well, there's a new pandemic starting, but Joey can give you immunity."

She laughed. "You have quite the imagination, always had since you were a child. How can a cat give me immunity to a pandemic?"

We were going through the tunnel into midtown. I didn't know how to reply, but I thought the truth, however weird, would be best. If I let Joey explain when she arrived at my place, she might have a heart attack. Better she thought I was crazy than that. "The people who took Joey were aliens from a planet called Felinedae, Their leader, Catling, kept Joey and other cats from Earth for eighteen months. During that time, they were fed certain foods and taught certain things to help us when the pandemic came."

Mother was silent as she absorbed this. I was waiting for another laugh, but she kept quiet until we exited the tunnel. "Quite a story, Lily. I think Kerri would love it. You should tell her when she comes with your sister today. She loves fairy tales."

I decided not to tell her the rest. She would have to see it to believe it.

When I helped my mother carry her bags into my apartment, Joey and Jezebel greeted me. Joey messaged me telepathically, "Is she ready?"

"No, not yet," I said.

Mother looked at me curiously. "What's that, Lily?"

"Nothing. Why don't you freshen up? You must be tired after your flight."

"I'm fine. When is Laura coming?"

I checked my watch. "She'll be here soon."

"Oh, good. I can't wait to see the baby and Kerri, of course. I'm sure they've both grown so much since I last visited."

I'd forgotten that my mother had yet to meet her new grandchild in person, although they'd communicated through FaceTime. "I haven't seen them in a while myself. I'll help you bring your bags into my room. Maybe you want to unpack before they come." Since there was only one bedroom in my apartment, I had promised Mother my room while I slept on the pull-out couch.

Mother laughed. "Are you trying to get rid of me for some reason? Are you hiding anything, Lily? I can tell when there's something up with you. It wasn't as easy with Laura, but you always had a hard time fooling me."

It was then that Joey started rubbing my mother's ankles and meowing. I was afraid he was about to talk, but he just made cat sounds.

"What does your cat want? Oh, this was the one that disappeared, the one you said is an alien." She bent down to pet him. Mother no longer had any pets. After she lost my father in 9/11 and her last cat a few months later, she never got another. She replaced them both with bottles.

"Yes, that's Joey, but I didn't say he was an alien, and you don't believe me, anyway. He may want to eat. Let me feed him, and you can put your things away."

"You're doing it again." Mother extricated herself from Joey and grabbed her bags. "I get the hint. Do whatever you have to do, Lily." With that, she carried both bags away and walked down the hall.

I turned to Joey. "Why did you do that?" I whispered.

"Excuse me, but I really do want to eat. That food you left out leaves a lot to be desired."

"I like it," Jezebel said. "you're too used to alien food."

"When do you want me to tell her?" Joey asked as I changed his and Jezebel's dishes.

"Let's wait until my sister and her family are here. It'll be easier that way, hopefully."

It turned out that Mother, after putting away her things (I'd left an empty drawer for her and room in the closet), needed a nap from her trip. While she slept, I began cooking dinner. Laura, never prompt and even less on time with a new baby, arrived a half hour late. Todd came in first carrying a highchair and foldable playpen with Kerri at his side. Kerri ran to me. "Aunt Lily. Wait until you see Toddy."

"Don't call him that," Laura said, entering with the baby who was already taking his first steps. She gave me a quick kiss on the cheek. "Your nephew is quite the roamer now, so you better watch out."

"I've tried to baby proof what I could," I said.

"Good. Is Mom here?"

"Yes, I am," Mother said, entering the room. I noticed she'd changed her clothes. She wore a pair of Jeans and a tie-dye t-shirt of rainbow colors.

Laura laughed. "Mom, you look like a hippy."

"I take that as a compliment." She took the baby's chubby hand. "This must be junior."

Todd said, "He's a big boy. I think he'll take after me in height." Todd was about six feet tall compared to Laura's 5'2."

As Todd set up his son's highchair by the table, Joey and Jezebel sauntered into the room. The boy exclaimed, "Kitteee," and went to grab his tail.

"Oh, no," Laura said, pulling his arm away. "Don't do that. Hey, Lily. Isn't that Joey?"

Before I could answer, Mother said, "Yes. He's back and, according to your sister, he's been with aliens on another planet."

"Aliens," Kerri said, her blue eyes wide, "Did they have a spaceship?" She didn't recall the day Catling landed at her house and took Joey. She'd tried to protect him and her own cat, Garfield.

Joey flashed me a quick message. I assumed it would be that he wanted to set everyone straight. Instead, he said "Turn on the TV. Quick, Lily."

My TV was in the kitchen, as I liked to watch it while I ate. I switched it on.

"What are you doing?" Mother asked. "That's rude, Lily. We're about to eat."

All the stations were broadcasting news. I watched as an image of President Young filled the screen. "Fellow Americans, I have amazing news to share tonight," she said, "Telepathic cats have landed on Earth and are immunizing people against the new COVID 3 outbreak by breathing on them. My cat, who'd disappeared from the White House eighteen months ago, returned today and gave me this news. She said she'd been taken to a planet called Felinedae whose leader, Catling, recruited her and other felines from Earth to help the human race survive this next pandemic."

There was a roar of questions from reporters. Young waved her hands to silence them. "I know this is hard to believe, but I have proof." She placed a cat carrier atop the podium where she stood and unlatched it. A Siamese cat strolled out. She picked it up and placed it next to the mike.

"What my lady says is the truth," the cat said in a deep voice. "I am JoJo. I am one of the cats who was chosen to save your world."

The crowd erupted in roars. Cameras flashed as they took photos of the President with her talking cat.

At the table, everyone had gone quiet. Mother finally spoke. "I haven't had a drink in one-hundred days, but I need one now."

Joey said, "I'll see if I can get that for you.."

I was glad I didn't keep any hard liquor in the house, but I had the leftover wine that Norman had brought. I stopped Joey before he could get to it. "Don't, Joey. She can't have any."

"I was just being hospitable. Can I tell them my story now?"

I switched off the TV with the remote. "Go ahead." He had the attention of the whole room. Laura's mouth was open. Todd was staring ahead blankly. Kerri was giggling, and the baby was banging his feeding spoon against his highchair tray.

Joey cleared his throat. It sounded like he was about to pass a hairball. But before he spoke, Jezebel jumped in front of him. "Move over, brother. Let me fill them in. I was actually the one Catling wanted, but I traded you and Jake so I could stay here with Lily. Her memory was wiped out with the other humans, so I had to tell her our story. I don't mind recounting it now."

"But you don't know what happened on Felinedae," Joey said. "I didn't tell you everything, and these humans like full disclosure."

She stepped back. "If you insist."

Joey told his story. When he was done, he delivered the breaths to everyone gathered except me and Baby Todd. Jezebel hadn't wanted the breath but was immune naturally.

Laura, who still looked dazed, asked, "Why didn't you blow on the baby?"

"There's a slight problem with that," he said.

I'd already assumed my friends and family would be protected, so it surprised me when he mentioned some difficulty. "What problem?" I asked.

"Sorry, Lily. I should've told you sooner, but I'm terrible in math. I can't even count my toe beans."

"I hate math, too," Kerri said. She was the only one who didn't seem frightened or confused by a talking cat.

"What does math have to do with the baby?" I asked.

"I don't have enough breaths."

"How can that be?" I counted the number of breaths he'd already administered to me, my three friends, and their three cats. He'd also given Kerri, Laura, and Todd breaths. That made ten which meant he had two left. "You should have two left, Joey."

"Two's not enough." The baby started crying. Laura took him out of the highchair and bounced him on her knee.

"I'm sorry, but young Earthlings need more breaths."

"I'm young," Kerri said.

"No. You're a big girl. It's kids under five. They require five breaths."

"So, what do we do?" Laura asked. "This is such a shock. I still think I'm dreaming, but, if I'm not, I want to know. I can't lose my baby." She glanced at me.

I knew that if Joey gave the baby five breaths, he would die.

"What if you give me one of your breaths?" Jezebel asked. "And Lily calls back her friends and has their cats give a breath. That makes four, and you'll have one to add which makes five."

"Nope," Joey said. "They have to be five breaths from the same cat, and only the cats who were on Felinedae have twelve breaths. The ones who were given the breath from a Felinedae cat only has one."

I didn't want to sacrifice Joey, but what could I do? I looked at my baby nephew in my sister's arms and felt tears form in my eyes.

"It's okay, Lily," Joey said, as if reading my mind which I'm sure he could, "We all have to die sometimes. I had a wonderful life with you." He walked over to Laura. "Put the baby back in the highchair. I'll jump up on the table and do the honors."

"No," Kerri cried. "I don't want the kitty to die."

Todd hugged his daughter. "It's the only way to save your brother, Ker. He's a brave cat, and he's doing the right thing."

Laura said, "I'm so sorry, Joey. This feels like a dream to me, a nightmare. I hope I wake up and everyone is alive and healthy, and there is no new pandemic." She put Baby Todd into his highchair.

As Joey jumped on to the tray, Todd walked over. "I can't believe this is happening either but, if it is, I owe you a big thanks for saving our son, Joey."

Tears began to flow as Joey prepared to breathe on Todd, jr. But just as he turned to face the baby, I heard a loud whirring noise. While my memory of the first encounter with the Felinedaes had been wiped out, I recognized the sound. Joey and Jezebel's ears turned back.

"Something's on the roof," Mother exclaimed, following their gazes.

"It's the spaceship," Kerri said.

A moment later, the apartment door opened and a six-foot tall cat walked through followed by Joey's brother, Jake.

"Catling! Jake!" Joey cried. He jumped down to greet them.

Catling said, "Greetings, Lily, and family. I've brought Jake home, so he can help Joey."

Jake said, "Hello, Brother. I just finished my training and am ready to administer the breaths." With that, he hopped onto Todd, jr's high-chair tray. The baby let out a giggle as the cat breathed on him five times.

Laura said, "I still think I'm dreaming or have gone crazy, but I feel much better."

"It's a relief," I said. "and now I have all three of my cats home."

"For now," Catling said as she turned toward the door. I watched as her long tail disappeared out into the hall. A few minutes later, I heard the sound of her spaceship returning to Felinedae.

ABOUT THE AUTHORS

KEVIN CATHY

Kevin Cathy is the author of many horror novels, short stories, and screenplays, many of which are written under various pseudonyms.

LAWRENCE DAGSTINE

Lawrence Dagstine is a native New Yorker, video game enthusiast, toy collector, and speculative fiction writer of 25+ years. He has placed more than 450+ stories in online and print periodicals during that two-decade plus span, especially the small presses. He has been published by publishing houses such as Damnation Books, Steampunk Tales, Left Hand Publishers, and Dark Owl Publishing (of which he has a new short story collection being released in 2023 called The Nightmare Cycle). He is also author to numerous novellas and two previous short story collections from the 2000s era: Death of the Common Writer and Fresh Blood. His work is available on Amazon and B&N.com. Visit his official website, at: www.lawrencedagstine.com.

DEBBIE DE LOUISE

Debbie De Louise is an award-winning author and a reference librarian at a public library on Long Island. She is a member of Sisters-in-Crime, International Thriller Writers, the Long Island Authors Group, and the Cat Writers' Association. She writes two cozy mystery series, the Cobble Cove Mysteries and the new Buttercup Bend Mysteries. She's also written a paranormal romance, three standalone mysteries, a time-travel novel, and a collection of cat poems. Debbie has also contributed to several Red Penguin Collection anthologies and their Bloom Literary Journal. In addition, she writes for Catster Magazine. Debbie lives on Long Island with her husband, daughter, and two cats. You can learn more about her and writing by visiting her website at https://debbiedelouise.com where you can subscribe to her blog and/or newsletter.

LISA DIAZ MEYER

ALL ROADS HOME, ALL ROADS DESTINED and ALL ROADS SHATTERED are New York author, Lisa Diaz Meyer's current works of award winning dark fiction. Readers can also find her short stories and poetry published in several Red Penguin, Nassau County Voices In Verse and Bards Annual anthologies.

For more info and links visit lisadiazmeyer.com

JOSH POOLE

Josh Poole is a visual artist and writer working out of a sleepy Virginia town. His work has been published in Air Mail Magazine, The World of Myth Magazine, and many others.

WILLIAM JOHN ROSTRON

William John Rostron is the author of a series of novels steeped in late 20th music and culture. Band in the Wind, Sound of Redemption, and Brotherhood of Forever have received critical acclaim from Writers Digest, the Online Book Club Review, and many other reviewers. These books have found readership on five continents and 47 states. On Oct 20, 2022, Band in the Wind placed in the Top 100 (out of millions of titles) in its genre in both the Kindle (#35) and paperback (#91) formats.

He has published more than three dozen short stories in anthologies, with five of them receiving awards from Writers Digest this year.

Most of these pieces have been reprinted in his short story compilation, A Flamingo Under the Carousel.

Five of his short pieces have been produced on the New York stage and are available for viewing on the author's website, www.WilliamJohnRostron.com. His short story "Pretty Flamingo" has been turned into a short film script by his daughter, Brittany Rostron. This script has won nine awards from Hollywood and New York film critics and is in the pre-production stage of the film process.

Born and raised in Queens, NY, William John Rostron now splits his time between his home on Long Island and traveling the country in his Tiffin motorhome. He is busy completing a bucket list of travel adventures when not writing. In the past 17 years, he and his wife Marilyn have traveled 125,000 miles. These journeys have taken them to the 48 contiguous states, 133 national parks, all 30 major league baseball stadiums, 154 cities and towns, two Canadian provinces, and various unusual experiences and locations. Many of these locations have served as backgrounds for his books.

He recently completed the first draft of his fourth novel, The Other Side of the Wind, and is working on his second compilation of short stories, T-Rex Stole My Computer.

JAMES RUMPEL

James Rumpel is a retired high school math teacher who enjoys spending a part of free time trying to turn a few of the odd ideas circling his brain into actual stories. He lives in Wisconsin with his wonderful wife, Mary.

J.R. RUSTRIAN

J.R. Rustrian loves to write stories as a hobby, getting inspiration from life, movies and games. He lives in Southern California with his wife and works in technology for a living. When not writing, you can find him cooking, hiking and going to the theaters. You can find him on Twitter @J_R_Rustrian

TRAVIS WELLMAN

Travis Wellman lives in NE Washington with his girlfriend and their cats. He has been published in The World of Myth Magazine, and in print anthologies The Dating Game Modern Romance Short Stories - The Red Penguin Collection, and Are You A Robot? - Three Cousins Publishing.

DIANA LEE WOODY

Diana Lee Woody is a writer, artist, and physicist. She writes short stories, stage plays, radio plays, and screenplays. She has produced, written, and directed award winning films and radio plays. She likes to add science to her stories whenever she can. Her favorite genres are sci-fi, comedy and horror. She is a native of the east coast, hailing from Silver Spring Maryland.

ALSO FROM THE RED PENGUIN COLLECTION

FICTION

What Lies Beyond – Sci-Fi Stories of the Future

I Can't Find My Flashlight – Contemporary Campfire Stories

A Heart Full of Love – A Collection of Romantic Short Stories

Behind Closed Doors – A Mystery Anthology

Once Upon A Time... – A Fairy Tale Anthology

Ernest Lived ...and other Historical Fiction Short Stories

Until Dawn – A Supernatural Anthology

Treat-or-Trick – Halloween Horror Stories

Pets On the Prowl – An Animal Mystery Anthology

My Robot & Me – A Not-So Fiction Anthology

POETRY

'Tis The Seasons – Poems to Lift Your Holiday Spirits

the flower shop on the corner – A Spring Poetry Anthology

the ocean waves – A Summer Poetry Anthology

the leaves fall – An Autumnal Poetry Anthology

Proud to Be – A Pride Poetry Collection

Words for the Earth – A Poetry Project

THE STAND OUT SERIES

Stand Out – The Best of The Red Penguin Collection, Vol. 1

Stand Out – The Best of The Red Penguin Collection, Vol. 2